UMBRA ISLAND

Volume one

The undying Saga

BY

AMBER E. BAGLEY-BENNETT

This book is dedicated to my long suffering family
And those who have helped me along the way
Including Julie Martin
and
Nicole Stokes

I have been told that spirits with unfinished business still linger around us, unseen or unnoticed by the living; but what if there was more than just the dead amongst us? What if other *things* were here? I had an aunt who believed in demons who could walk amongst humans and they would do as they pleased. Superstition was all around me. In this year, 1885, people are obsessed with the supernatural world and it being part of ours. Fortune tellers peddled their fake truths on every corner of London gaining their money through fear of the unknown.

I do not believe in any of this, at least I did not. Here amongst these pages be mindful of what you read. Darkness comes in many shapes. My darkness is an Island. Yours will be my words.

HW

14/09/1885

The firm called me into the office today. A strange occurrence as I was about to start my leave of absence. It was not often that Mr Wilkes was in the London office and even more unlikely for a basic lawyer like myself to have a face to face meeting with him. After only four years of work with them it was all but unheard of in point of fact.

I hate to admit it but my chest wobbled with nerves when I stood outside his door. The hat shuffling between my fingers must have happened once too often as the young Secretary offered to take it from me. I can't say it helped my nerves to not have it or to do so.

"Mr Whitman, it is good to see you!" Mr Whilkes extended a hand to me, having appeared from a door behind me; I shook it and we entered his office.

"Err, thank you sir."

"Tell me, how is your family? I hear you recently lost your father?" He enquired, closing the door, the lock clicking into place.

"Yes sir, um, last spring, consumption, I'm afraid. We had not seen each other in some time before that. Just myself and an aged aunt who has an affliction of the mind. I dare say by today she will have no recollection of me." I wasn't sure why I went into so much detail. Still the old man listened like he was truly interested.

"These are harsh times we live in, lad. You are a family of some wealth, if memory serves me. Your father held a large account with us, did he not?"

"He did, sir. It all came to me upon his death." Why was he so interested in me?

Mr Wilkes nodded his head and planted himself firmly behind his desk, gesturing for me to also sit. His great frame only just squeezed into the wooden chair without force; I found myself focusing on the way his waistcoat bunched around the armrests.

"Well, that is enough of the pleasantries, don't you think?" I grinned, a breath of a laugh coming out at his words, "Time is valuable for both of us. I have a job for you. It is a large account that needs a lot of work, they have not had any accounting done by professionals since this Duchess took the role. The family has been with us for longer than the company has had a name; the first client of the Wilkes family; and unfortunately, has been long neglected.

They are a very prestigious family, Duchess Whetton's estate. Have you heard of them?"

I had to think for a moment. "A vague memory of the name from my school days, sir. Relations to our Queen are they not?" I sat up straighter in my chair.

"Of a sort, yes, it could be put that way." Mr Wilkes simultaneously brushed his white moustache as he handed a large file across to me.

"I see they live in the South." I said.

"As south as you can get before you become French." Mr Wilkes laughed.

"How long do you require my stay with them?" I asked, not entirely sure where the island mentioned as their address was. He took in a deep breath through his nose, visabally filling his lungs.

"Until the job is done, lad. The Duchess is looking to renovate her home, it has not been done in many years and she would like to bring the old manor into the modern era. Add electricity to the main house, that sort of thing. You will overlook the renovations whilst you get their ledgers into order. Any resources you need can be ordered, through the firm. I am told there is a small cottage set aside for you on the estate. It may be smaller than you are used to, perhaps you should have your belongings downsized and delivered to you there." He paused, stood and moved to the window. Looking down at the busy London street below, he took up most of the window casting a long shadow across the floor. Mr Wilkes lit a second match, his pipe refusing to burn.

"Coach and ferry tickets are in the file you have there. The firm is putting our trust in you, my lad. Our reputation rides on your success. Any missteps with this account could be the end of us all."

"Yes, sir. I appreciate the opportunity you are giving me, but are there not more qualified men for the job?"

He turned back to me.

"I have been watching you, Mr Whitman, you have impressed me. I have pushed for you to have this role," he rounded the desk, "you are the exact man for the job. I know it."

"I shall leave tomorrow." I stammered the words, held under his tight gaze.

He shook my hand once more as he opened the door for me. The secretary handed me my hat; a sad sort of smile on her face. I pushed that to the back of my mind.

Upon returning to my apartment in Kensington, I took a moment to speak with my landlady. Mrs Hobbs was a delightful older lady who always gave me kindness, a friend of my mothers from a long time ago. She gave me an extremely decent price on my monthly rent. I welcomed the hug she gave me.

"It is such short notice, I will transfer an extra month's rent to your accounts to cover any vacant time." My firm ran her accounts so it would be easily done. She waved her hand at me.

"Psh nonsense, just take care of yourself." she insisted as I walked towards the stairs.

Looking around the second floor apartment, part of me was sad to be leaving my humble accommodation. After so many childhood years living between the eight bedroomed family home and my boarding school it had been a peaceful change of pace to have only two rooms. I packed up the few things that would travel with me and emptied my wardrobe into my old school trunk before sitting down to some supper. I flipped open the file to read about the family I had been charged with.

For the last two hundred years only women had been born into their bloodline. Meaning only women had held the duchery. Something about that tickled my humour, what a way to foil the patriarchal world we live in, and with a queen ruling England as well. I enjoyed the thought of women being in charge, suited to their natures. Perhaps I will not admit that to my male peers just yet.

According to the file the Duchess has a father and an aunt who live with her in the main house, along with a household staff of five. The land staff was not enclosed. The Island sits just off the coast of a port city. A navel port mostly from what I have heard. Though this Island was new to me, I had little knowledge of Portsmouth. I was sure I had never seen the Island on any maps before. The Isle of Wight I knew but not this one, the map in the file showed it clearly though. I wrote myself a note to enquire at the library for its history first thing in the morning.

The daylight has all gone now and I am sitting with little light as I write. I saw this notebook on my table, an unused last gift from my father. I remembered what my mother once said to me. 'Write it all down' whenever we did something of note she would always write it down in her green book for us to look back upon. I had always meant to do it, but after her death it got harder to do so. There are a great many things I meant to do before now. Well now on this adventure I will write down as much as I can. There may be some details of the family I must keep out, but I shall write. Perhaps I shall even send some pages back to my employer. I know Mr Wilkes will want frequent updates from me about more than just their finances.

A feeling swept over me, one I had not felt since I was a child. As if someone was watching me from the dark corners of my apartment. I felt it as I changed out of my suit and into the night shirt sliding into my bed before writing these notes. No, I am alone.

I should sleep. I have a long day tomorrow.

Good night

Where do I start with my day? It has been, well, interesting.

Mrs Hobbs woke me early, far too early given my late night. There was a man at the door with a letter for me. His knocking had awoken the whole house eventually. The Cossell sisters told me how sickly the man appeared, as if he had been ill for many years. I only half believed them, the way I only half believed they were really sisters. Two young women living together with no sign of family or suitors seemed suspicious to me. Still their arrangement was none of my business.

The letter informed me that arrangements had been made for the collection of my things to the estate and a private carriage would be waiting for me at three pm in hopes of arriving in time for the last ferry. I have tucked the letter into the back of this book so I will not forget it or lose it.

With that information in mind I wrote notes on what was to be taken and what should be left behind for Mrs Hobbs safe keeping. Per her request.

The need to never appear unkempt to an employer took hold, so I walked my way to the barbers for a haircut and a shave. Yes I could have shaved myself but I have the disposable money in my account. It had been a long while since I had a hair cut. I asked for the most modern of trends which took my dark hair up away from my ears and waxed on the top. It fit neatly below my derby and no longer caught beneath my scarf. The barber made sure that I bought a tub of the wax he used as well so I would never be without the *right look*.

On my way out I bumped into Hamish, an old school friend who had also started working for WIlkes around the same time as I did. "I hear you've been given a new assignment?" He laughed

"News travels fast." I said as we walked together.

"They have given me some of your clients. Wilkes works fast." We both chuckled for a moment. Hamish seemed hesitant to ask about the Duchess, his family had been employed by Wilkes for generations so I was not surprised he knew of the account.

"It's been a long time since any one was sent to the Island. My father wouldn't talk about it." He told me. "He just said you would need your wits about you. Father said you can never let them twist your thoughts." He gave me an odd sort of look, "whatever that means. Father has been hitting the liquor hard recently." Hamish was trying to laugh it off. I could see there was a twinge of something else.

The rest of our time together, which was not long, was awkward and silent. Eventually, I bid my friend a farewell, agreed that on my first opportunity I would return and would empty the tavern of its ale.

I have to say in the time since gaining this assignment I have had the oddest interactions with people. Even the librarian gave me a strange look and a warning when I asked for a book on the Island. He told me there was no such place and turned me away. I wondered for a moment if I should reconsider my acceptance of the job, there had not been much opportunity for me to think it over, to consider any of the consequences of going to this unknown place.

Breakfast went by with very little incident. I filled the silence by reading more on the family. The first Duke had been given his title by the king of the time for his efforts in the army. Helped of course by the king being his cousin a few times removed. There is a story of an argument not too long after between the two men on a cold, thunderous night. An argument that resulted in the Duke being sent to the Island. Not much of consequence happened for many years until the Duke's death. His only child, a daughter, took the claim to his title. The death is still a mystery to doctors and scientists alike. Books tell of a rumour that he had died long before the official date, years in fact. I wondered if the family's own archives would shed more light on the matter, though I doubt I will get a chance to look too closely. I continued to read right up until lunch was placed in front of me.

"Last meal here, Mr Whitman. I am no longer your housekeeper or landlady." Mrs Hobs giggled. Sitting across from me and resting her chin on her hand.

"Perhaps still a friend, Dear Mrs Hobbs." I took hold of her hand in mine, she squeezed it.

"Always a friend, dear. You will keep in touch won't you?" I nodded.

"Of course, the first thing I will do upon arrival is send a telegram of my safety to you. I could never have you worry."

"That is right you will. I will worry for your safety every hour I do not hear from you." Tears welled in her eyes.

"Mrs Hobbs, please don't fret. I will be well looked after." I assured her.

We ate our meal together, going over my luggage, ensuring I had all I would need straight away and packing anything she felt I had forgotten. In honesty I have to admit I am going to miss her fussing about me. The old woman fusses about all her tenants. She truly does love every one of us like her own family.

By three pm I had my coat on and had moved my luggage to the main entrance of the building. The carriage arrived precisely as the clock chimed the hour. The driver wore a large hat and black coat. The combination made his face almost impossible to see. I glanced only two cold blank green eyes, blank yet somehow scowling at me. I silently hoped he did not reflect how all the staff would be at the Duchess' house. He was unceremonious with me speaking only when needed to, asking very little questions and giving short answers to any I asked him.

I blew out my cheeks in mocking frustration towards Mrs Hobbs. We bid our last goodbye to each other at the door and I waved to the Cossell sisters, standing in their window. Both dabbed their eyes with hankies. I laughed to myself, endeared by their sentiments.

The shutting of the carriage door felt final in a way I had not felt since childhood. A finality like I was leaving London forever. Forever had not been part of my vocabulary for many years, so it left a bad taste in my mouth. One that I am yet to rid myself of as I write this.

All that could go wrong with our journey appeared to be in line to do so. First our path was blocked by a fallen tree, barely out of the city and nature had stopped us. My driver insisted that I not help the other men who struggled. He said that we should be ready to leave the moment the road was clear. I understood his thoughts, still that was not part of my nature. We soon made light work of the old oak, managing to push it aside the road, enough that coaches could pass by comfortably. I hadn't noticed straight away but a large splinter had stuck in my left palm in the fleshy part next to the thumb.. Not wanting to slow my already exasperated driver I ignored the pain. Wrapped my handkerchief about my hand once I was back inside the carriage.

The driver whipped the four horses into a full charge to make up time I assume. I was shaken around so fiercely I felt as though I was dancing a particularly energetic jig in a crowded tavern. I felt every bump we rolled over. One even bounced me entirely out of my seat. I knocked on the roof of the carriage asking for the speed to lesson. My request was ignored. The horses were puffing, upon looking out of the window I could see how they foamed at the mouth

"Are you sure we should keep going at this speed?" I called up to the driver. My heart stopped when I saw he was no longer in his seat. Panic struck me. What could have happened to him? My heavy overcoat dropped to the footwell before I opened the door to climb out. I took a moment to assess my path to the driver's seat. Of course as I reached for the top an overhanging tree branch swept across my back, pulling my body away from the frame, my splintered hand losing grip for a moment. I was sure I was about to fall. Willing myself to hold on I grappled to gain as tight a grip on the metal bars as I could, pulling myself up onto the roof. For a moment I stayed lying there catching my breath, and regaining my bravery until another bump in the path reminded me of our plight. I clambered over to the driver's seat. Caught the reins and pulled them back hoping it would slow the horses. The biggest of the four horses reared upwards causing the carriage to falter. Below me a wheel buckled against a rock on the road, it did not break fully and continued to turn. The pull on the horses caused them to slow and I was able to catch my breath.

We had all but lost the light as we pulled into the seaside city of Portsmouth. The gas street lamps were few and far between on the outskirts of the city, yet were all that lit our path to the shore. I was not a knowledgeable person on pathfinding so we got lost a few times. Eventually we reached the beginning of a fast ocean. Seeing the promenade explained to me why even our Queen enjoyed holidays here. I pulled up, climbed off the carriage and entered a tavern. I was told no such ferry was in place to travel to the Island I sought. No one ever went to the Island. Another man warned me not to go there at all. I declined their offers of a bed for the night determined to find my way to my charge as promptly as they wanted. With no luck inside I went back out onto the street. There I discovered a woman standing beside the horses, smoothing the large one's nose. At first I thought I could see all the way through her. The material of her dress, the hand that moved across the horse's neck, was almost blurred. She looked back at me.

"Ahh Mr Whitman, you are behind schedule. Where is Marcoff?" She spoke with the authority I had only heard in keepers of the grand houses; her whole body coming more into focus as she spoke.

"Marcoff?" I asked.

"The driver we sent with this carriage."

"Oh, I am not sure, he made haste with the horses and then made a hasty retreat from his post without my knowledge. It was somewhere this side of Wickam that I realised his absence." I said , pulling my overcoat from the footwell and sliding into it.

She sighed, "I will send out a search for him. Come with me, our boat is waiting.

I nodded, noticing that my luggage had been transferred to a small cart pulled by another man, from what I saw he was a port worker and nothing to do with my new employers. The carriage of my adventures was driven away by yet another cloak covered person. Our journey across the water was mostly uneventful. We boarded a small schooner which made easy work of the calm water of the English Channel.

Mrs Lipton, my new companion and the housekeeper of the Duchess' house, explained that the lateness of my arrival has meant I will have to spend the first night in the main house. We entered through the servants doors so I saw little of the house itself except the dark corridor which led to my room. It was not in the servants quarters though, the room reminded me of my father's old bedroom. I will describe it tomorrow when I see it in the light.

I should sleep, the day has been long.

16/09/1885- am

Unfortunately I found myself utterly unable to sleep due to the pain in my hand. I had done well to hide it from Mrs Lipton. I wish I had not done so. Unwrapping the handkerchief revealed a lot of blood drying against the material and my skin. Holding onto the reins on the carriage has caused the splinter to travel deeper into my skin and the blood to seep out. It had to be washed and removed, I knew it, before I could go any further with its healing. So I grabbed the empty water jug and ventured out of my room.

A few candles lit the corridors, high on the walls. They led me down to the kitchens, I spared no time to check the decor of the house. In hindsight it might have been a good idea to do so, given my reasons for being here. When I entered the kitchen a woman was sitting half turned away at the table, her hands wrapped around a china cup.
"Oh I am sorry, I did not realise anyone would be awake." I said quietly.
"You're not a bother, Mr Whitman." She rose to her feet, "I apologise for having rushed you to us the way we did."

I blinked. "You are the Duchess?" I asked.
"Yes, but please call me Cassandra." She stopped, looked down, spotting my hand, "Oh, what happened?" Cassandra asked gently, taking my hand in hers and examining it.
"A fallen tree and four racing horses, I'm afraid."
"Here, sit down, I'll pull it out for you." I did as she asked, watching her move around the room. Cassandra grabbed the kettle from the stove and poured some out into two bowls.
"Put your hand in this one, it will soak some of the blood away. I think the cook keeps a sewing kit around here, there may be some tweezers we can use...ahh yes, here we go." She pulled a round tin box from a draw. The Duchess sat down beside me, placing the sewing box on the table

next to the bowls of water and a cloth she had found. I pulled the burning candle on the table closer to us, giving more light to the situation. Her hands were soft on mine, turning it into the right position, slowly wiping the dry blood from my skin.

"I was not looking to be seen by the lady of the house; especially when that lady is a Duchess." I tried to keep my voice steady

"Nonsense, you are hurt, that fact comes before any social status either of us might hold. Now stay still, this could hurt a lot." The duchess placed the cloth into the second bowl of water, shuffled about in the sewing box until she found what she wanted. For a moment she placed the end of the tweezers into the flame of the candle until she was satisfied, I clenched my teeth while she pulled back the skin on my hand and slowly pulled the wood from my hand.

"This is more than a splinter, Mr Whitman." She was not wrong. The shard of wood was at least an inch in length and it had some girth to it. Cassandra used a bandage she had found to wrap my hand cleanly. Our eyes met.

"Mr Whitman, we are very pleased to have you here. It has been a long time since we have had anyone from the Wilkes company here with us." Cassandra spoke quietly, looking into my eyes.

"Yes, um, at least sixty years according to the files."

She dropped her eyes back to my hand that she was still holding.

"Yes, before my time and yours. My father, of course, was still young himself."

There was a shift in her breathing as she spoke, "Well my tea is cold and you have had a long journey today. We should both retire to our rooms." She stood again, passing in front of the globe lamp on the far side of the room. I saw then that her night dress was transparent in the light. I am not embarrassed to say that I looked at her body. She was slender in places; neck, forearms and waist, yet she curved in all the parts that delighted my sensibilities. I found myself nodding as if agreeing with the instinctual voice telling me to enjoy her. It was my turn for my breathing to change, speeding up. I cleared my throat and forced myself to turn away from her. I grabbed up the jug I had brought down with me and headed to the door, opening it and waiting for Cassandra to finish replacing what we had used.

On our way up the staircase she took hold of my arm instead of holding the bannister. Our eyes met briefly for a moment and I noticed how blue her eyes were. So blue, in fact they looked almost white in the low light.

We reached my door and she bid me good night. I opened it but stayed in the threshold as she walked away, her long red hair skimming her waist as she went. I watched until the Duchess had turned into the dark corridor. Once more I had to force myself back into my body, content to watch the space she had occupied so briefly. I pushed my door closed behind me, leaning on it for a moment, then put myself to bed. I have awoken in plenty of time to write this entry before breakfast. I look forward to finding what else this day has in store for me.

I was awoken by the maid knocking on my door. She had a note for me, which she placed on the bedside table before moving over to the fireplace and stocking the fire with new logs. I sat up in my bed, watching her.

"Please do not treat me like one of your employers. I am just a lawyer." I implored her. She looked up at me, a small smile on her face.

There was no answer from her so I unfolded the note. It told me that I was expected for breakfast by the Duchess and her father. I met Mr Whetton at the door. He was a tall man, much taller than I, slim in the face. His dark hair had begun to grey at the side and had grown out past his ears.

"Good morning, Sir." I said.

"Is it a 'good' morning?" He rolled his eyes, taking a seat at the table.

"I am sorry, sir." I sat at the setting across from him, "Will the ladies of the house be joining us?" I felt silly asking.

"I suspect the Duchess will come today. She will want to introduce herself to you." Mr Whetton lifted his newspaper from the butler's tray, unfolded it and disappeared behind the sheets. I know that was a cue for me to stop asking questions, yet I had more of them.

"And your sister, the Duchess' aunt?"

An audible sigh came from the man. The butler informed me that Lady Anna is unwell and almost never attends meals, as she has been confined to the East Tower, alone.

"Thank you, Mr Lipton."

The door behind me opened letting the Duchess in. She was already dressed in a grand green gown. the like I had only seen at balls. The green showed off her pale skin exquisitely in the autumn morning light. I caught my breath and licked my bottom lip. She spoke to me with a smile, as if we had never met.

"Welcome to our home, Mr Whitman. It is a pleasure to have you here."

Confused, I kept up the charade.

"Thank you, your Grace. I am pleased to be here. The change of pace from London is very welcome." I took her lead and began to add food to my plate.

"We are, as you can see, very much in need of an update in the decor here. I would like to start with the main entrance and the ballroom."

"Perhaps we could let the man at least eat his eggs before you give him your orders." Her father huffed still behind the newspaper.

"Of course, how silly of me," She giggled, "Our cook is wonderful, you will enjoy everything he makes." Cassandra smiled at me, tapping my arm lightly.

"I am sure I will, however I do have simple tastes, your Grace."

Quite to my surprise Mr Whetton slammed the paper down, threw his chair backwards, and tucked the newspaper under his arm. His lips were pulled tight and he breathed through his nose, short sharp breaths. I was unsure of where to look. Was this act for me or the Duchess?

"What is wrong with you, Charles?" Cassandra tilted her head to one side. Looking at her, his eyes softened and he let out a sigh, his fingers twitched at his sides.

"I think I will take a walk." He nodded his head to me, then darted from the room. Cassandra lowered her head.

"I am sorry, Mr Whitman, Charles, My father, he can be - well I fear he is headed in the same direction as my aunt. He is beginning to age as you see." she said.

"Yes, my own aunt has a disease of the mind." I was trying to comfort her, "She hardly recognises the nurses she sees daily. Her whole attitude is different and I no longer see the sweet woman she was." I couldn't stop myself talking, telling her about my aunt's illness would not be helpful.

"It is closely similar to my aunt. We try to keep her away from guests, for her own mind. You will think me ghastly but with her delusions it is imperative we keep her as calm as we can. I think, Mr Whitman, if you do not mind I will leave you to your breakfast. I have had Mr Lipton prepare all the books and financial information in the library for you."

I nodded, rose slightly off my chair and watched her walk to the door. Her demeanour was so different from the night before.

"Um, Cassandra?" She stopped and looked back at me, "Call me Horatio please."

A smile that didn't entirely reach her eyes acknowledged my request before she left. I sighed and sat down, ate the rest of my eggs and filled a plate with toast before I made my way to the library. It was not as large as the one in London, yet the books. The books were old. Older than I had ever seen, large and bound in leather. I was immediately desperate to read every single one of them. That would have to wait, a job was at hand. It was there I spent the rest of the day, alone and working.

This is far more work than I had anticipated. It has taken me three days to even locate the entire balance of their accounts. The family owns land all over the country in fact all over the world. Their largest estate was held in Egypt of all places. A home likened to the pyramids in its grandeur and housed hundreds of people. All had once been homeless vagrants, now housed and given work. In Norway a village owed its commerce to the family, again housing them almost rent free. So many countries and so many poor families having their lives bettered by them. I was awed by it. All in all with the land and money held in banks my new employers had no need to worry about their spending. As it stands on this day they have a net worth of seven hundred million sterling pounds. More than the royal family. I had never thought I would see such wealth, let alone be the holder of the accounts. I wonder if the family have a superiority complex? Do they feel themselves better than all others? Do the natives of these countries, these towns the Duchery have built really feel such love for them? Or is it simply the story portrayed to the English masses to keep the royal family in good stead? Is this my own misgivings of the British wealth coming to the surface? I could not fathom how a single family could obtain such vast riches.

I spent the last part of the day sending out letters to contractors around Portsmouth. Cassandra wanted to throw a ball in two months; so the work had to begin immediately and be done fast.

In the last few days I have not seen the family much at all. Mr Lipton, the Butler, had been bringing my food to the library. I can't help but wonder if breakfast that first day had something to do with it. I have now moved to the small cottage I had been promised. It sat on the edge of the main house's gardens. I have been told that it once housed the original gardeners' family. In all honesty it feels nicer than in the main house. The oppressive feeling of anger didn't linger over every room. However, there is still an odd feeling around me, as if someone watches me wherever I go. The only room I truly feel alone and safe is the bedroom. It is small and has only a twin size bed in it. Still holding the mattress with ropes. Yes, call me vain and spoiled but I have always preferred the room to move when I sleep. Is it vanity or left over from a breeding problem? I hate to say it but my family's background is not the most humble. I slept in a full size adult bed at the age of three and my room could have housed the cottage twice over.

I digress, my attention span this evening has been non-existent, I try to concentrate at least on this journal. Perhaps I should -

I apologise, I do not know what it was that I was going to say before. A knock at the door distracted me from those thoughts. The maid had brought a letter to me. An invite from a man in Portsmouth. At first I was confused by the invitation until I saw who my host would be. Mr Wilkes, the same name as my firm. I assume he is part of the company as well, so I have taken tomorrow off to accept the invite. The maid, her name is Lilly, I believe took my reply. She warned me not to tell the Duchess where I was going, or who I was meeting. A strange request, still I complied and have made further arrangements to meet with a contractor in the city centre.

As I left, the feeling of being watched returned. I looked over to the collection of small clipped trees. A shadow of a man stood there, his arms folded over his chest. His presence went unnoticed by the maid. I shut the door, turned the key and rushed up the stairs. A strange feeling really, to be scared by the unknown. It is leaving me now. I am tired.

With that said I will turn in for the night.

I had forgotten today would be a Sunday. It is easy to forget the days on the Island. The streets were quiet with many people attending the numerous churches. The schooner had brought me to the opposite side of the shore line, a less built area with fewer houses. The captain of the boat told me he would collect me promptly at four pm. If I was to miss the boat he would not return until the next day. A fair word I dare say.

I pulled out the note and followed the directions to a town house just off the main high street. The housekeeper answered the door and led me out to the garden in the back. Upon seeing me the man jumped to his feet.

"Ah Mr Whitman, Welcome! Come, we are just having some tea. This is my wife Ramla."

"Pleased to meet you Ma'am." I sat opposite the woman.

"Now there is no need for pleasantries." A family trait to the Wilkes, I saw, "I have asked you here today for one reason." The new Mr Wilkes said. "We implore you to reconsider this employment on the Island." His face was serious.

"Mr Wilkes I apologise but I cannot. I have already agreed and my belongings are in transit."

"Mr Whitman, call me James. It is imperative for your safety to please return to London. I will compensate you for any money you will lose." He reached a hand over to mine as he spoke.

"James, with all due respect, unless you have the authority to fire me from the firm, I have a job to do and once my word is given I will not take it back. I see this is a matter you feel strongly about. I assume a family feud for your choice of marriage perhaps. It is none of my business, my business is to run the financial accounts and all legal matters for the Duchess. Thank you for your hospitality." I bowed my head to the lady, already feeling the bad taste in my mouth for my words.

A dark hand clasped my arm as I reached the door. I turned to face Ramia. Her soft hand came to rest on my face.
"You are so young, younger than the others." Her eyes were sad, "I can see you are a man of integrity. Our feud with the Wilkes family and the distrust of the Duchary runs old and deep. If you will not listen to our warnings perhaps you will at least look into these." Ramala handed me a small note, I nodded.

I couldn't say no when she begged me to stay for at least a cup of tea. She led me back to the table where James had already poured out three cups of tea. We drank it with milk, no sugar and talked about local history. I had been unaware of the amount of famous people who had come from the little city. Even the great king Henry viii enjoyed spending time here and built the castle by the shore. I lost myself in the conversation until sometime later when the sun was clearly across the yardarm. I left the town house and walked down to the contractor, I was running the risk of being late. He reluctantly agreed to work with me though I did have to raise the amount he would be paid a significant amount. Of course not a matter for the Duchess' finances. All the comments and fears of the Island were beginning to make me question the job all together.

At four pm on the clock's strike the schooner came to shore, I watched it sail over. I climbed in and sat down in the same spot I had done so the last two times. Not one of the small crew spoke to me as we crossed the water. I watched the island shore come closer, a cloaked figure waiting on the dock.

"Looks like you are highly favoured, for a lawyer." The captain sneered at me. I didn't fully understand what he meant. Then she lowered her hood and Cassandra smiled at me.

"Will you take a walk with me, Horatio?" Her voice, it felt comforting to me as if I was returning to my family. I took her arm in mine, following her lead across the damp grass.

"Did you have any luck with the contractors today?"

"Yes actually, they will arrive in one week to commence work. You will be dancing the night away in your modern ballroom before you know it, Your Grace." I answered, strangely feeling the need to bring back a formality in our conversations.

"Oh wonderful, I have so longed for gayity to come back to these old walls." Her eyes glanced back at the house nostalgically. We walked in silence for some time until we eventually came close to the main house. A song drifted out from the East tower. It was like an angel called down to me from heaven itself.

"My aunt, she sings so beautifully doesn't she?" Cassandra stated, moving herself into my eyeline. I forced my eyes down to her.

"Yes, though she seems sad, almost." I said.

"She laments." The Duchess told me that her aunt sang of happier times, when her mind was not as fogged over as it is now. All while moving me away from the house.

"There is a rumour, amongst the people in the city, that we captured a siren and kept her locked in there. They say she calls out to the sailors who will come to us and save her though all die trying." Contempt filled her false laugh.

"We live in a world of such technological advancements yet so many still hold onto the old superstitions." I had seen some of those superstitions in the last week.

"I keep asking Charles, my father, to move her to a different room. It saddens me that she looks out over the grave yard every day. Our whole family laid to rest in the one place dear Anna has to look over." She gestured to her right. A small hill rose with an iron fence around it. My eyes looked over the stone monuments then up to the tower's windows. A faint shadow moved away from the glass.

"I weep for her." Cassandra caught my attention back to her once more. I noticed then how she tried to hide a dark bruising by her eye with make up and her hair. Unthinking, I brushed back the red locks. She cowered away from me.

"What happened?" I grabbed her wrist to pull her back to me.

"It's nothing, I am very clumsy at times that is all." She turned away.

"Is this why you so infrequently have guests here and why I have been kept away from you in the last few days? Who did this Cassandra?" Each word came out more stern, she would not look at me. "Cassandra, please!" I lifted my hand on her shoulder begging her to look at me.The tears in her eyes turned them icey blue.

"Horatio you cannot help me."

"You are the Duchess, there is no one here who could put their hands on you."

"Your eyes Horatio, your eyes are so kind. It has been such a long time since I saw such kindness."

I thought for a moment. I had to find a way to protect her, the conclusion came to me, "Your father did this, didn't he?" She did not outwardly agree, yet I knew.

We have come up with a plan. She does not think Charles would be as inclined to harm her if another man was in the house. Therefore, this evening I will cause a series of inconvenient leaks to burst throughout the newly installed plumbing around my cottage. The damage will happen late enough that they will have no choice but transfer me back to the main house. Where I will begin to take up more of Cassandra's time discussing the renovations. Yes it is the perfect plan. I could not see such a beautiful woman harmed.

Perhaps this was the real reason Cassandra has asked for the presence of a lawyer to live within the grounds.

I cannot think on what could have happened had I not arrived.

On my way home that evening I walked down through the gardens. It was a quiet walk with many blooming flowers. I marvelled at the skill of the gardener to have so many in bloom at this part of the autumn. I quickly reminded myself I knew next to nothing about gardening. To be honest these flowers could be doing exactly what they are supposed to do and I would never know.

I rounded the corner to my cottage and stopped abruptly when I saw them. The Butler and Housekeeper were walking together. Mr Lipton stopped and picked a rose, sliding it into his wife's hair. Her smile was wide and full of love as she slid her arm round his and rested her head on his shoulder. No words needed to be said between the two of them; the love between spoke every word they needed to hear.

The plan worked. I am in the main house and luckily because of my family name I have been situated in a room not far from the family quarters. A different one to my original, but in my opinion far better. This one was almost straight onto the staircase and consisted of three separate rooms, the main room which held a large canopy bed, a desk and seating area. My own bathroom came off one side to the left of the room with a dressing room attached. It was easily larger than the cottage. I was extremely delighted with the room, knowing forwell that my presence here irked Charles.

Supper yesterday was awkward. Hardly a word was spoken between us all. Though Charles did show an interest in the renovations, once we retired to the parlour after eating. He asked if we had planned on where the workers would stay. An odd question to me, I had thought that he would know of the workers quarters.

"In all honesty, sir, the contractor insisted the workers be housed off the Island and not in your own employee accommodations. We agreed on a residential building close to the seafront." I said.

"An extra expense to my daughter's bank accounts." He looked directly at her when he spoke.

"I agreed to it, *father*." Cassandra interrupted.

"I assure you sir it makes little difference to the accounts." I said.

"You have it all worked out I see. My thoughts are unneeded. I shall leave you to it then. Cassandra, it has gotten late, you should retire soon."

She nodded at him then turned to the fireplace. With a clearing of his throat and a sigh, Charles left us alone.

"Why do you not send him away, Cassandra?" I stood behind the drinks table. Cassandra took in a breath, pain of memory evident in the way she clenched her jaw.

"Our family is regal but we are banished to live only here. Whilst the world may come and go across the water we are, by law, not allowed. Even those who marry into our bloodline become one of us. Including our punishments."

I didn't really understand, nevertheless, I could see pressing the matter would upset her.

"Would you put the gramophone on? It is so quiet in here this evening."

I complied, how could I not? I felt her body behind me, almost touching me.

"Will you dance with me?" She asked. I took hold of her hand and clasped my other around her waist. The smell of lavender rose up and filled my nostrils. We danced slowly, not quite a waltz and she looked up at me.

"How old are you Horatio?"

"Twenty seven." It sounded too young in this room.

"And not yet married?" She almost laughed.

"Work and my father's illness took my time." She gave me another sad smile.

"And you Duchess, how old are you?"

"How old do I seem to you?" She replied.

"It is hard to tell, you have the youth in your skin, a youth that longs for knowledge, yet your eyes and your mind, they hold a deeper wisdom; one beyond this world."

"After my mother's death, I had to grow up quickly to perform my duties as Duchess."

"Of course, and no husband has been..." I didn't know how to finish my question.

"No husband. Men have asked but none have been what I wanted to be with forever."

A wave of braveness swept over me. I bent down, kissing her red lips. The lavender scent engulfed me. When I felt her kiss me back I wrapped my arms around her body, pulling her into me. It was as if we had been made to hold each other this way. I lifted her up and sat her on the side table, running my hand up to her face.

As suddenly as I'd kissed her, Cassandra pulled away from me, whipping herself across the room. Both of us tried to catch our breath. I lent my hands on the side table and lowered my head.

"I am sorry I shouldn't have-" She cut me off.

"No. We need to be careful, control ourselves as much as we can." Without another word she left the room, leaving me alone. I sunk into a chair confused in my mind and my body frustrated. Candles began to be put out around me.

"The Duchess is intoxicating is she not, Sir?" Mr Lipton chuckled.

"I'm sorry?" I frowned.

"Men cannot resist her charms. The Duchess enchants all that meet her."

"She does."

He stopped abruptly, turning his full body to me and stepping close.

"If you will sir, I have placed a book in your room. You would do well to read it."

Confused, I thanked him and made my way up to my room. WIth the scent of the Duchess still lingering around me and a portrait of her opposite my bed I - satisfied - my wanting need.

Today however was mostly uneventful. I worked in the library by myself until midday when Cassandra came in. She sat with me for two hours as we went over the designs for the ball room and entrance hall.

I am sorry but I cannot concentrate any longer on my words. Anna is singing again. It is beautiful.

I need to see her.

I woke up very much confused this morning, more confused than I had been thus far. Last night I had left my room, made my way towards the East Tower, the solemn song calling out to me, to something inside of me; like the siren song Cassandra had spoken of.

I knew the door should have been locked, yet it stood ajar, a gentle breeze swept over me when I pushed it further open. The dark staircase led to a small dim light calling me upwards. My feet moved as if they had trodden the steps many times before, easily avoiding the creaks and breaks making no noise.

At the top I saw her standing at the only window, a veil draped over her face and hair.

"Hello? Anna?" I whispered, she spun to face me, lifting the veil over her head. Why, she wasn't old at all! In fact she would match my own age beautifully.

Through a whispered voice she asked me to sit with her for a moment. A small couch stood beside the fireplace. Our legs touched as we sat. We talked about the slowly worsening weather as autumn had begun to approach us. Anna asked to see my hand. Her touch matched the softness of Cassandra's, perhaps softer yet.

"You do not seem the way they say, why do they keep you in here?" I asked.

"Jealousy. The Duchess is jealous of my face. They keep me in here so no man will want me over her and turn the head of suitors. They lie about me to keep me away from anyone who might want me."

"I don't understand, Cassandra is so nice."

"It's an act," She waved me off.

I am not sure what really happened in the next few moments. I felt a weight holding me to the chair. Anna licked the healing wound on my hand. It stung for a moment, my vision blurred. I felt myself being laid down. Lips on mine. My body moving and replying to her touch but without my consent.

The cold air hit my chest when my shirt was unbuttoned. Anna bucked and writhed above me, it felt good to my body, every nerve below my skin was on fire. Yet in my head I knew this was not right.

My eyes rolled as she kissed me once more. Everything was dark. There was only her body against mine and her voice whispering in my ear. Her skin was on fire under my fingers.

"I heard you two nights ago, smelt your happiness. Now that happiness will be mine."

"No." I could only muster a whisper myself. I tried to move, to push her away but cold steel touched my throat. Movement had all but left me. The blade moved to my chest where it began to slice through my skin. My eyes opened fast seeing the once young Anna now older, her face grey and lined with age. Her teeth are what I remember the most. All of them, too many, too long and too sharp. Her hair bellowed out behind me.

I fell into more darkness. A voice I vaguely recognised, then nothing.

I awoke today. It was mid afternoon. My throat and chest are hurting more than I can describe. So far no one will tell me anything about what happened. I have seen only Charles and Mr and Mrs Lipton. Charles who wanted only what I could recall. The Liptons saw to my fire, food and wounds. I asked every time they came in. Each time I would be palmed off with an excuse.

"I want to see the Duchess."

"She is dealing with greater matters right now, sir. She will be along when the time is right."

All day I have drifted between sleep and confusion. What happened to me? I feel utterly dirty in my own skin, it is no longer my own flesh. I am trapped beneath it.

Too many days have passed. My head still spun when I stood but today is the first day of construction. I had to welcome the contractor and his workers. I set them to their jobs and retired myself to the day rooms.

My first glimpse of Cassandra in days came this morning when she finally joined me.

"I am sorry for my absence during your recovery, but my Aunt was so very frightened, she was out of her mind. The intruders had her tied up in the closet."

"Intruders?" I asked

Cassandra poured me a cup of tea that she had brought in with her.

"Two men and a woman. They were going to kidnap her. The poor woman has barely slept in days and what they did to you. That despicable woman tried to...the way she cut into you and used a drug on you." She put her hand on my knee, "you do forgive me don't you, Horatio? I wanted so much to come to you."

"Of course, I do." Her smile was infectious and I matched it with my own. She lent herself forward planting a soft kiss on the side of my mouth. There was no lingering touch.

"My father will be out tonight if you'd like to have dinner with me?" She asked.

"I thought none of you were not allowed off the Island?" I shifted myself away from her, my body wanted no one's touch.

"No we cannot. There is a problem with the stores on the south side of the Island. Charles has volunteered to help the men with it. He said he would be gone for the night, perhaps even most of tomorrow as well. I thought it would be a fine opportunity for me to fully show you around the house."

My brain told me to refuse the offer. Told me to return to my room. Yet I was agreeing before I had realised.
"We could start now?" I asked.

She walked me around the lower grounds, through the orangery and several rooms my father would have approved of. Each room she opened with a key she held on a chain attached to her skirt. If I am honest with you and myself, I liked the rooms and the house. There has always been a part of me that missed the finer side of my father's money and even now that it is mine I forget the fact. I especially missed the way my mother had dressed our home, at least what I could remember of it. I visited so little as I grew older. I ignored how she would skip rooms all together.

We moved upstairs and I really began to look at the house. The paint was peeling from the walls, portraits hanging in broken frames. It was clear the place had not been touched in many years. The damage was worse in the dark corridor that led to Cassandra's bedroom and the way to the east tower. I could feel the dampness in the walls by just looking at it.
"I know it is terrible in this part of the house, still every Duchess has slept in this room since their arrival here, you see." She tried to justify it to me.
"Then the moment the ballroom is completed we will begin work here and nowhere else. My Duchess must have only the best!"
"Your Duchess?" She grinned up at me.
"Ahem, yes I, I suppose as I work here now and will be for the foreseeable future you must be."
"I like it, I will call you my lawyer."

We laughed for a moment. Down stairs the noise of men clattering about with wood and metal ladders tried to distract us. None of them really mattered, the miad tiptoed past us as no more than a shadow. I hardly noticed any of it. For me all there was, was the smell of lavender drifting off Cassandra to me.

The low light we stood in married with the beams of light that fought through ripped curtains showed me why I felt the way I do. The beauty that stood before me was triumphant for want of a less flowery way to put it. The green of her dress complemented the red of her hair in a way I had not experienced before. Nore did I understand it. She broke my fantasy by moving away further down the corridor. A shadow against the window seemed to slip back out of view as she approached it.

"We should make my Aunt's room nicer as well, perhaps the men would be kind enough to do so?" She asked, stopping at the door that in the daylight I did not recognise. The air was colder and thicker in front of that door. Everything in me wanted to either dart away from it or rip it open.

"I thought perhaps you would like to see Anna, settle your mind that she is safe." Cassandra held a large key upwards. How could I say no to this? Duty and curiosity pushed me onwards. The stairs seemed steeper this time, each one creaking with our weight.

"Anna dear, you have a visitor!" Cassandra called up the steps. I heard a squeak of a wheel. The Duchess moved aside at the top of the stairs showing me the frail woman in the wheelchair. I swallowed a lump that had formed in my throat. Cassandra crouched beside her.

"Aunt Anna, your saviour is here." The man who fought those ugly thieves away. Mr Whitman."

Vacant eyes shifted over to me. I felt a pull in my gut that had me walking forward and dropping to my knees.

"Anna?" I asked. The eyes, it was definitely the right eyes I had seen that night, her skin though; it was not what I knew. Still soft but wrinkled by age.

"The poor thing has hardly slept. Aunt, you remember this is the man who saved you and fought off the men who tried to hurt you." Cassandra got up and began to pour a cup of tea for the old woman.

Anna raised a hand to my face, I anchored myself to the ground, not wanting to flinch away. Her fingers smoothed up into my hairline. There was a flash of light behind my eyes, blinding my vision for a moment. A metallic taste rose up in my mouth. All went black around me. Before my eyes closed I was sure I saw Cassandra lunging forward with the kettle.

I woke up again sitting up against Anna's bed, Cassandra sitting next to me.

"Oh Mr Whitman, you're awake."

"What happened?" I asked, rubbing the back of my neck.

"It was Anna, she lunged at you. I had to pull her off. She is settled now, I think she thought you were one of the intruders. I have gotten her to sleep, the poor woman. Come on now, can you stand?"

I took a few breaths, nodded and allowed her to help me up; before we left for the stairs I took a glance back. Anna was lying back in the wheelchair, her head limp to one side. I could not be sure but I thought I saw a rope around her wrist. Cassandra walked with me back to my room.

"You should rest." She said. I agreed, reluctantly. She promised to have Mr Lipton oversee the work until I am well again.

"Sleep well, my lawyer." She grinned.

"Thank you, My Duchess." I looked once more towards Anna's door, "She is okay?" Cassandra audiably sighed at my question.

“She will be fine. I will call for the doctor again. Now,” her hand pressed against my chest, “Get some rest.”

I nodded, pressed a brief kiss on her lips, and breathed in the lavender scent. I waited for a moment, holding her to me. From somewhere else in the house the housekeeper called out to her, beckoning Cassandra away from me. I closed my door and fell into bed.

I cannot be sure but I am convinced I heard voices last night. It may have been a dream but I heard some of it. I think I did at least.

"He still suffers from her effects." A female voice said.

"Then you must double your efforts, your Grace." An older woman replied.

"Anna slept with him, simple kissess and the perfume will not be strong enough to break her hold." A man said.

"I can't do this again." the first voice said.

"You must, for the house and for them you must." The man sounded much angrier this time. "It was your parents who caused this, their daliences in Egypt that wrought this curse upon us. You must do your duty and keep the blood flowing."

"You must make him love you, make him stay here, the pretence must be kept! Use your body if you must, but make him yours." The older woman demanded.

The rest of the conversation was a blur. I woke up again to the sunlight on my face. With a sigh I stood and moved across to the vanity table. I looked at my face, stubble was growing fast. Odd for me, as it had always been so slow to come. I did not sport a moustache like most of my peers as it took far too long to become anything more than fluff on my lip. I ran my hand over my face feeling the coarse bristles scrape against my fingers, then drifted down to the small cut on my chest. It was healing well, though I still felt foggy as to the cause of it. My hand too was doing well, it had not bled for sometime and the wound had begun to scab over.

I decided I would venture into the city, see a barber and perhaps have a look around a little. The dockyard held many ships of historical value that I had not seen before. Any excuse to leave the Island for a few hours seemed good enough for me. I made sure to speak nothing to the schooner captain but instead used the ferry that had brought the workers over that morning. A cold wind whipped from the sea through every street of the city making me wrap my coat collars tight around my neck; kicking myself for leaving my scarf at the house.

As quickly as I could I darted to the city library. The workers there all whispered to each other when I passed them. Clearly they knew where I had come from. My coat had hardly left my shoulders when a stout older man dropped a large dusty book in front of me. I thanked him through my confusion. The book looked like it hadn't been opened for years. The pages were so thin my fingers felt like they would tear through them if I turned too fast. It was a history of Portsmouth, a blue ribbon marked the page meant for me, The arrival of Duchary.

It told me that the Island was originally attached to the mainland via a bridge. At first it seemed the city, which at the time was still a relatively small port town, all trusted and loved the family. They would hold grand balls for the poorer people in the town and their staff would be given the night off. For many of the young women and men it was a dream workplace. It all seemed to be too perfect. Sketches of how the house looked then was so eerily different to the one I have been staying in. It seemed that it had once been so full of light and love, every room open and inviting. The gardens were bright and blooming. I couldn't fathom how it could have changed so much.

I don't know how long I had been sitting there reading, it felt like minutes to me, yet when I finally looked up the library was busy and I was hungry. I threw on my coat quickly. As I tried to hand the book back the librarian told me to keep it.
"It will help you more than us."

I thanked him with a breathy laugh, still confused, and turned to the exit. Mr WIlkes, the Portsmouth Mr Wilkes was standing in the doorway. I sighed.

"Lunch, Mr Whitman?"

We went off to a local restaurant where James insisted on paying for everything.

"I hear the renovations have begun. Are they going well?" he asked.

"In all honesty I am not sure. A few days ago something happened, a break in." I went with the story I had been told, even if I didn't believe it. The look James gave me, ha, I knew he did not believe it either, "Some men attempted to kidnap Anna. I managed to stop them, but alas I got hurt in the process so I have been absent from my work."

James' face fell as I spoke.

"You were with the aunt? Did she touch you?" His eyes swept over me. My mouth was drying out. I looked at my hand, the feeling of her coarse tongue still there.

"No, no she didn't." I lied, "James, you aren't telling me everything you know are you!"

"Mr Whitman, you must return to the cottage and look within the bedroom, the fireplace is your best bet. It can tell you much better than I can."

I grimaced, "There may be a slight problem. The cottage is, well there was a problem. I am in the main house currently."

James lowered his head and sighed.

"You must be careful. Keep your wits about you. I will send help for you. Trust no one on the island. Your life may depend on it." He was suddenly frantic, throwing money on to the table and pulling me out of the restaurant.

"Do what you must to keep yourself away from the aunt."

"I don't understand any of this, James." I was almost begging him to help me understand.

"The rumours about her are truer than any of us would like. Keep your wits about you."

I nodded as James scuttled away. Yes scuttled, something about those tiny legs made me think of bugs running from the light. I started back for the Island, the library book tucked beneath my arm when I remembered why I had come to the city. I found a barber and had the stubble shaved from my face. The hot towel he placed to soothe the skin gave me some peace. The barber spoke to me, I know he did and I answered, well I think I replied. I cannot be so sure now to be truthful with you. My mind was so fixated with the Island, on Anna. What really happened that night? My memories, they were all so confused and mixed together. I had to be sure. I wanted to reread this journal. See what I said before the lies were pushed into my mind.

I have no idea if I was polite to the barber once he had finished, I was so desperate to get out of there and back to the Island.

At the port no one would help me. Every boat refused to take me across the water. Eventually I found an old man sitting beside a row boat. Leslie agreed to sell me the boat. I gave him a note to send to my employer who would pay him one hundred pounds for services rendered. He was agreeable to that and he pushed me away from the jetty. I silently sent a thank you to my school teachers for taking us out on the river so often. I should have kept up the workouts each row of the oars pulled on my shoulder muscles as they tried to remember the rhythms.

I stopped when I heard it, as if it had broken any power to move. My head snapped instinctively to the island shore. The source of the song. It was Anna, I knew it was. That same blue dress and veil she had worn that night. I could not understand the woman I saw in the wheelchair could not have walked so easily as she was.

The song echoed out across the water and shook my chest. I took up the oars once more altering my path to meet her. I kept my eyes on her. The tall slim body gliding over the grass. I couldn't get to her fast enough though I tried. I couldn't stop her as she stepped into the water. I knew the boat would be slow. I stood and dove into the water. The cold of it shocked my body for a moment. The song, now under water, was pulling me onwards.

"Where is she?" I said out loud. Something brushed my foot. I spun. A face in the water.

It was Anna, I knew her eyes but her face was wrong. Too cold and too grey. Still that song was, it was perfect. All my heart, mind and body wanted to hold her, no matter where we were. Taking in a deep breath and pushing myself down under the water. I put my hands out to her and we took hold of each other. Her face came close to mine and our lips touched. I pushed the last of my air into her mouth, she had to keep breathing. Her hand around me clamped down harder on my shoulder. I tried to pull us both upwards to the surface. The current was stronger than me. It had to be the current pulling us down, it couldn't be her.

I thrashed my legs against the water, they were no longer knocking against her knees but hitting a singular hard force. Something that wrapped itself around me clenching my body. Stopping me from moving.

We were sinking further down. My chest was tightening and gasping for air. This wasn't right.

As I flailed and fought against this deformed Anna, I was sure I was done for. Part of my brain silently made peace with this death as my lungs strained against the lack of oxygen. Several flashes of light shot through the water. Was it real or was it my mind shutting down? Anna screeched, the sound was deafening. She fell away from me. Hands grabbed me. There was so much confusion as people ran about shouting. I briefly saw the row boat being pulled up the shore by the butler.

With my book tucked below his coat he and Mr Whetton dragged me up into the house. I tried to ask what had happened but neither would speak to me.

Finally they left me alone again. I sat at my desk and wrote this down. I know no matter what else happens on this day I had to write this down.

Her eyes were gold with slits of black instead of rounded, yet somehow still familiar. Her hair bellowed out behind her in long black streaks. Anna's skin was grey, almost translucent in the water. Her hands webbed to the middle knuckle. Where legs once were, now a tail; like a snake's body had wrapped around me.

I know this all sounds ridiculous. I am not sure how I knew it. A picture of her was in my mind as if a portrait had been placed before me. My head feels foggy in a way. I should sit by the fire for a moment. Get out of these wet clothes.

Is it hot in this room?

That song, so sad.

Mr Lipton gave me tea to calm me.

Is the fire lit? I'll douse it.

Should I sing back?

Are you there, are you listening?

It could be cold. Is it cold? Do you see them? Feel them? Watching you? The men I see them in the graveyard every day. Standing amongst the graves.

I should write to Mrs Hobbs

That singing. How is she singing? What is she?

There it -

02/10/1885

I was drugged. According to Cassandra I was drugged that day in the city. We have no idea who could have done it.

Cassandra has hardly left my side, the reason for my absence from this journal. It has been delightful. Yes, I have been confused about the whole situation. Confusion appears to be a constant for me now. Yes, I have been questioning it all. Still having Cassandra with me has been comforting.

She often holds my hand when we sit together and she holds my arm when we take a turn around the gardens. The ongoing works on the ball room and entrance hall are going well. Cassandra agreed to donate the old furniture to less fortunate families in the city. She wanted to make me happy, which it did. Very much so.

Her hand feels so soft in mine and always, the smell of lavender surrounded us. For some time today I simply sat and watched her read a book. Until around eleven am when the family, including the butler and housekeeper went down to tend business on the far side of the Island leaving the maid and I alone in the house with Anna locked in her tower.

I decided to take the time to have a wander about the house by myself despite feeling weak. To my disappointment most of the rooms were locked up, keeping me out. After the fifth locked door I slumped back against the wall, Lilly shuffled quietly into the kitchen with armfulls of white sheets. I followed her in.

"Is there something you need, sir?" She asked, looking up from her work.

"No, no please, I was just looking around, but the rooms are-" I gestured in a way to finish my sentence.

"Yes, the Duchess is very particular about that, what with the builders in and out." I saw the moment she caught herself. There was a fact she was not telling me.

"Of course." I agreed with her, then crossed the room to pour out a cup of tea. Behind me Lilly shifted the envelopes on the table.

"I am not supposed to hand out the post, it is Mr Lipton's duty, but here; you should have these now." The young girl handed me a set of letters.

"How old are you Lilly?" I held eye contact with her as I pushed the letters into my jacket pocket.

"Twenty, sir."

"How long have you worked here?" I asked.

"My whole life. My mother was the maid here before me. I always helped with her duties so when she died I took over." She sunk down into a chair as she spoke.

"I am sorry for your loss, how long ago did she leave us?"

"Twelve years ago. I was eight." Lilly sat for a brief moment almost lost in thought.

"Where is your father?" I hadn't been really interested at first, yet now the nervousness in her face pushed at my curiosity.

"I am sorry sir, I cannot talk about this." She quickly darted for the door. Unfortunately I was closer, taller and faster.

"No." I grabbed her shoulders and spun her to face me. "Your eyes, they are just like his. Cassandra's father. Charles is your father isn't he?" I couldn't tell you why I had made the connections. Her eyes, yes they were similar in colour to Mr Whetton, yet nothing she had said truly pointed in his direction. Perhaps I have read too many novels. Tears had rushed down her face.

"Sir, please."

"Tell me, Lilly. Is Charles your father?" With quivering lips she agreed, nodding her head. We stood there for sometime, with her thick cotton dress creasing below my hands. "Your mother, what happened to her?"

Her face gave me every answer I needed, wide, deer like eyes, fear, regret and sadness. "They killed her didn't they?"

Lilly continued to weep, I pulled her into my chest, cradled her head in my hand.

"I'm so sorry, people like them, with titles and money, they can be the worst type of people. They have no care for others." Her breathing staggered against me as she began to calm down. Holding her tiny body against mine felt good in a way that was different to holding Cassandra's. She had no overpowering scent, her clothes and hair were simple and soft. It was refreshing to me and truly the first time I had felt comfortable touching another person since I first met Anna. After a few minutes the maid pulled back from my chest, realising herself from my hold.

"I am sorry, sir. I should not place myself against you. Not when the Duchess is so keen on you." I looked over at her face. She forced a smile.

"Sir." Lilly rubbed her fingers against her palms before wiping them both on her apron.

"I'm sorry. You may go about your work, Lilly." I cleared my throat, quietly. She bowed her head and gave a small curtsey to me. Her small feet could not have carried her out faster unless they had been equipped with wheels. I sighed and slumped heavily against the kitchen wall. An action I find myself doing more and more recently. My eyes locked with a pair across the room. A pair of eyes that had no body to hold them, dead eyes just staring at me. My mouth ran dry and my brain was stuck on them. No other thoughts could take any control. Fear spread through me like fire.

Mrs Lipton entering the house through the servants entrance broke my attention away from the eyes. My chest loosened, though a different fear now filled me, as quietly as I could I slid out of the kitchen and darted back to my room. I shut the door as quietly, trying not to let the clip make any sound.

I sat down at my desk to open the letters. I read the first as I caught my breath.

*'My dear boy, It was a delight to hear from you last week. I do hope
that you will find the time to visit us.
Stay safe, Yours Mrs Hobbs.'*

The second;

*'Mr Whitman, it is with sadness we write to you.
As of this week your employment with the Wilkes
financial services has been terminated. However we
are happy to announce the new contract of your tenure
under the service of Cassandra Whetton, Duchess of
Islington. The Duchess has agreed an increase to your
weekly pay, giving you one hundred English pounds
per week. We hope this is agreeable to you.
A lump sum of one thousand English pounds has been
credited to your accounts to recover any resulting losses
during the change over period.
The Wilkes company and family thank you for your
years of service and wish you well in your future.
Kind Regards
The office of Mr Wilkes.'*

What? I never agreed to this. I would have to speak to Cassandra when she returned.

The last envelope had no letter, only a key. A label had been tied to it.

Open every door.

I tucked it into my waistcoat pocket. My eyes had dropped into my hands. What is happening to me? This house, it is like the house is alive. Part of it speaks to me, pulling me into its comfort. The comfort of a young woman in a pretty dress. My mind is sure that it is wrong, that what has and is happening to me cannot be right. Still , I am compelled to stay here. It is clear to me now that Charles is a very dangerous man. My brain fought against my heart that ached to save the Duchess and Lilly.

I wondered if Cassandra was aware that her sister was working alongside her. I had to do something to stop him.

A memory appeared in the forefront of my mind. Mr Lipton telling me about a book. It had been weeks since then, the damn thing could be anywhere. I checked every tabletop in the room, knowing forwell if it had been left in plain sight, Cassandra would already have seen it. Defeated, I sat on the edge of the bed looking out the window. My view looked out over the water across to the city. It seemed so far away from me as I sat there. Portsmouth was almost tainted for me; knowing that I had been drugged by someone I thought to trust. The butler assured me that it had to have been someone who was close to me that day. The barber, the librarian, the people who cooked and served my food at the restaurant or even James Wilkes.

I am disgusted by the thought of any of them putting a mind altering drug in my body. Anna? I started to think about her again at that moment. She too had been in the water, but she couldn't have been drugged as well. There had been no singing since that day. A new courage rose up inside of me. I decided it was time.

I tried to slow my breath so it could not be heard and tiptoed to the dark corridor. Green and black curtains pulled over the single window at the end to cut out the light. I looked up at the ornate arches and ceiling moulds, wondering who had thought spiralling spikes and eyeless grotesques had been stylish decor. My breath finally blew out loud in a puff of visible vapour. Cold running up my back, making all the tiny hairs stand up all over my body. Slowly I slid the key into the door, remembering to push slowly so it didn't creak. A voice telling me to stop echoed in my mind. I stepped cautiously up the stairs. I ascended into the room my memory found familiar.

I was alone, no one else appeared to be there. The bed had been made with a mustard yellow comforter that matched the colour on the walls. Everything just a little faded. I am unsure why, but I had to touch the sheets. They were deceivingly soft. Hm, not a thing I often think about, the softness of sheets, they always had been in my mother's house and then with Mrs Hobbs. Impulse leading me my hand ran up the sheets to the pillows, pushing them down, testing the density. A feeling came over me of wanting, unsatisfied lust. My vision blurred into a memory as laid down on the bed, closing my eyes. The memory was like a dream coming back to me. I felt the hands that had once smoothed over my skin, burning now through my mind. Sweat poured across my forehead. My hand ran down and fisted the sheets.

Just as my mind began to relax into the euphoric feeling I glanced at a portrait on the bed stand. The face staring back at me was Anna, the clothes, she couldn't be in them. Not unless... the portrait was of her sitting out in the front yard, with an only half built house behind her. It had to be an ancestor, right? Or perhaps a costume? A painting over an old....not a photograph, it could not be. I grabbed the frame and looked closer. It was paint, the whole portrait was painted. I pulled the frame back and away to see the signature on the bottom left corner. It was dated: **03/03/1726**. My breath came out staggered. Uneasiness shivered through me, I didn't want to be there alone anymore. Was I breaking some unwritten rule by being up there?

Before leaving I took a look out of the window and saw someone standing in the graveyard, I couldn't see him properly as a blue glow surrounded him. I darted down the stairs to the corridore locking the door behind me. I whipped back the torn curtains hoping for a closer look at him, the graveyard was empty. I told myself it must have been a trick of the light in some way. I am still trying to convince myself of it.

Down stairs Cassandra was returning to the house. My heart sped up, jumping into my throat. I could see my bedroom door open. It wasn't too far. I could get there quietly and unseen if I timed it all right. I pulled the curtains back into place as best I could, then pressed myself close to the wall and moved slowly on the carpeted area of the floor.

I slipped back into my room and sat back in the armchair, breathing slowly; trying to calm my heart. Footsteps were coming up the stairs.

"Oh Lilly! Where is Mr Whitman?" Cassandra asked, Lilly must have hesitated because her answer took some time to come. The steps got closer to my door.

"Horatio?" She knocked on my open door and looked inside. I looked up from a book I had grabbed seconds before.

"Ah, you're back! I didn't expect you for a while longer."

"Yes, Charles is going to finish the work for both of us. I, well, I was missing you. I thought I would keep you company."

There was no way for me to refuse her. If I had she would know something was wrong. So, I agreed, put my book down and said I would meet her down stairs in ten minutes. When she left again I jumped back to my feet. I wobbled for a second, my sight blurring. My equilibrium soon righted itself and my light headedness dissipated. The key was heavy in my pocket so I pulled it out. Looking around I quickly ruled out several hiding places. Charles and Cassandra both knew the whole house better than I do. The bed! I noticed it some time ago. The frame has a lip on the underside below the mattress. I got down on the floor and slid the key under there. As I was about to get up again I noticed a book tucked right up in the corner of the bed. I made a mental note to pull it out when I had time.

  With a lump in my throat I walked down to the entrance hall to wait for Cassandra, tucking my coat under my arm and holding onto my derby.

"Tell me Mr Whitmen, my Lawyer, do you have clothes fit for a ball?" Cassandra as she walked up to me. She had emerged from a room below the staircase that I had been unaware of until that moment.

"Ah, no, I am afraid not, I don't have much time for balls as a lawyer." I laughed, my smile only faltering for a moment.

"Well that just won't do. The tailor and seamstress will be here tomorrow. Let me have a suit made for you. No, no arguments, Horatio. I long to see you in a cravat." She looked up at me through her eyelashes as she corrected my tie.

"All right, Cassandra. I could not refuse you anything." I relented.

"Of course you cannot, I am your duchess after all." Those eyes have become so easy to get lost in, and I did. The ageless eyes that appeared to know more than they should pulled me in. My face slowly moved closer to hers, her breath grazed over my lips. Once again the scent of lavender filled every sense. Our lips touched and all I could think about was her. My hand wrapped around the bottom of their face round the nape of her neck. Her hands clenched around my waist, we pulled each other closer.

Just when I thought our kiss might go further a commotion outside broke us apart. I threw the door open. The heat hit us hard. People were running back and forth, all of them shouting. I grabbed a man by the shoulders.

"What happened?"

"The stables are on fire!" He shouted at me and pushed away. Both of us darted in that direction. When we got there half the building was on fire. White smoke was rolling over the so far untouched side of the roof. The heat was everywhere, in the waves in our eyes and the pain on your skin.

With a glance back at Cassandra, I rushed over with everyone else. I could hear the horses still inside. Panic struck me, I had to help. As I went to run forward a hand pulled me back.

"No Horatio, don't!" She begged me.

"I have to." I pushed her back, "Stay here."

Ignoring every instinct in me I rushed into the burning building. The heat was more than intense. More than anything I had ever felt. I looked around me, trying to see through the flames and smoke. I tied my handkerchief around my mouth and nose, I pushed on to the screaming horses. Have you ever heard a horse scream? It's a noise that rips into your soul.

The metal on the first stall was red hot, my skin was burning before I even touched it. I ripped it open. The horse bolted past me.

I kicked at the other stall locks until all the horses were free, all except one. It had been tied to the wall with several chains. Though the pain in my chest I climbed over the door making eye contact with the large black horse. I put my hands out in front of me.

"Okay buddy, I'm here to help you, it's going to be alright." He was rearing up, eyes wide and foam dripping from his mouth. I finally got close enough to touch his neck and stroke him. "Shhh, now, it's okay."

I couldn't budge the chains by hand. I had to find something else. Amongst the now crumbling building I found a metal bar. I used it to separate the links in the chain. The horse reared up once more, kicking me back and pushing me to the ground. My head smacked against the brick wall and I slumped down. I watched as the horse kicked his way through the chained stall door. Hands grabbed at me, dragging me back through the fire out into the courtyard. I laid there staring at the sky, as people fought to put out the flames around me.

The length of time I stayed there is truly unknown to me. Mr Lipton and Cassandra helped me to walk back to the main house. I sat in the library for some time. Cassandra had Lilly clean my head wound whilst she went upstairs to change out of her singed clothes. I wanted so much to talk with the maid about that morning. The words would not come out properly. I took hold of her hand, looking up into her eyes. The only thing I could ask was - "Am I in danger here?" With wide eyes she whispered
"We all are."

03/10/1885

I don't know what to do any more. Yesterday was a lot. I am still trying to process it properly. One thing I am sure of is that I need to be out of this house. I asked if my cottage had been finished.

"You want to leave me?"

"Of course not, Cassandra, but my brain. This has been too much for me. I need some time, alone. A few days, by myself. With everything going on here, the building work and now the clean up of the stables. Duchess, I need time to recover."

"I understand. I will have Mr Lipton check on the cottage." She said.

All I could do was wait and pack my things. I slid the key back into my waistcoat pocket and the book from Mr Lipton I hid amongst my clothes.

I paused writing this for a moment. The focus on my own words were becoming too much for me so I went down to the library in hopes I would find more history on the family.

"Mr Whitman, I wonder if I might have a moment of your time?"

I spun round.

"Mr Whetton, of course, shall we sit?" I said.

"Hgm, it will not take long. I am told you are returning to the cottage shortly. Once you are settled I would like to speak to you about my will and testament."

I was surprised that his request was actually about my real job. I nodded to him.

"Yes sir. I will gather the paperwork." I replied. He moved closer to me.

"This must stay between the two of us. Not even the Duchess can know. Do you understand?" Charles' eyes narrowed.

"Yes sir, client confidentiality is important to me. Even if the Duchess is now my employer."

A strange short breath came out his nose before he left me alone again. I stood still for a long time, watching the space he had occupied moments ago. My mind was unsure what would happen if I moved too fast or too far. The air was still thick in the library, the smoke from the fire had come in through the windows. I looked around myself, wondering if the books could see me.

The wills were kept in a safe at the back of the library. It was hidden behind a bookshelf that moved forward if pressed correctly. I had been given access to it for the deeds when I first got here. It was normal for an in-house lawyer to have access to all the family's documents, so there would be no questions if I was found looking through them. To be honest, I was unaware in-house lawyer were even still an available job. The extremely rich could do whatever they wanted I suppose.

I scooped up the wills in the safe, tucked them into a large book before scooting back out to my room.

Not long after lunch Mrs Lipton escorted myself and my small amount of luggage to the cottage.

"Mrs Lipton, was Marcoff ever found?" I hadn't thought about my driver in a long time, still that figure at the graveyard had made me think about him.

"Unfortunately, yes. The poor man had been set about by thieves on the road. We are lucky they got only him and not you as well. The beggars killed him. Such a sad ending to such a loyal man."

The sentiment did not appear to reach her true emotions. I thanked her at the door and insisted I needed no more help from there. The old woman was reluctant to leave me at first, I could see it in the

way she glanced repeatedly at my things. When at last she left me alone
I sunk into the couch and let out a long breath of relief.

05/10/1885

I spent most of yesterday settling myself back into the cottage, the fire had been burning consistently since my arrival back here. It is cold, the September weather was still mostly warm outside, my bones had taken hold of the cold. I wonder occasionally if I will stay this way forever.

I sat watching the horses galloping about the fields outside my window this morning. They had been put out since the fire, their lungs being allowed to breathe fresh air after inhaling so much smoke during the fire. Only one of the twelve beasts had lost its life that day. The Vet had told Cassandra she had been lucky in that fact. I wasn't sure if luck had taken any part of the actions that day. Charles is sure the fire was set on purpose. The thought that anyone would want to burn thirteen horses to death was beyond my comprehension. I am of course aware that these crimes do happen, hell in London people do all sorts of horrible things to each other. I was never surprised by the heinous nature of humans, still I could not always understand why they would do them.

My chest still felt tight from the smoke and the doctor had been visiting me twice a day to test my breathing. He doesn't seem too worried at all, not even about my severe lack of body heat. I mention it each time he comes. It was only the first time that he made any reaction, his eyes glancing at Cassandra for a brief moment. I doubt most people would have noticed the look. I am trying to ignore my own feelings on the matter and follow his rule on it; after all he is the doctor.

Whilst watching the horses I spied Charles walking down the path towards me. I moved over to my desk to fish out the Wills from the locked draw. I felt an uneasiness sweep over me when I held them. It was as if I was doing wrong against the Duchess by keeping a secret I was not fully privy too. Behind me Charles was knocking on the door. This seemed odd to me, though I couldn't tell you why at that moment. I let him in and we sat on either side of the desk.

"I have reason to believe that I will not be around much longer. I last wrote this Will over thirty years ago. I feel it is time I rewrote it to include my child." He said, his formality had still not warmed to me.

"Of course, sir. I have the paperwork here, we can fill it out now." I grabbed my pen, dipping it into the ink pot. I know many people have begun using the steel pens with ink wells inside them, but I have always loved my dip pen. "Okay Mr Whetton, your own personal accounts hold fifty six thousands pounds and two deeds for homes in Yorkshire. The Bevlin Estate and Brinners House. I assume you wish to leave these to the Duchess?" I knew full well he had not been thinking of the Duchess.

"No."

"No?" I raised my eyebrows to him. Our locked eyes broke with the knocking of the door.

"I asked Mr Lipton to join us today, as witness to my signature." Charles let the Butler in himself. Mr Lipton sat down on the couch in silence.

"Shall I begin, Mr Whitman?" Charles did not change his facial expression at all.

"Yes, please do." I smiled.

"I wish to give *all* my assets to my daughter, Lilly Mayheart." He paused for my reaction, though I kept a straight face. Many years of training have ensured I show no emotion to what a client may tell me.

"You know about her don't you? That the maid here is my daughter?" He asked.

"Yes, sire, I worked it out a few days ago." I said.

"I am worried for her, should history repeat itself, as it so often does on this Island. I will not let her suffer the same fate as her mother," I caught the break in his voice, "My assets must be given to her and she *must* leave immediately to Yorkshire upon my death, or serious illness. Do you understand, Mr Whitman? *You* must be sure she is safe." For the first time since my arrival I saw true love in his face.

"At least you be kind to one daughter." I said before my brain realised it.

"Mr Whitman, you should know that I have only *one* daughter. I have no stepchildren, nor did I take the Duchess as a ward. I married as a younger man, not much older than you are now. My heart has never belonged to this house, or the woman I married. It was magic that held me here, the magic of this Island that took hold of my senses and takes hold of yours every day you are here. I am now an old man and I have outstayed my welcome in the house. This cottage is the best place for you to be. Everything you need to know about this Island is right here, if you only take heed of it."

Charles and Mr Lipton signed the Will, thirty minutes later once we had secured all his property. With the wax seal of English law I sealed the papers shut, ensuring no one would look upon them until his death. Before the two men left they watched me place the old Will into the fire. Satisfied it had been burnt beyond any repair they left me.

Nothing else of note happened today, I stayed in the cottage beside the fire, heated my own soup for dinner and watched the sun go down. A yellow, orange glow spread out over the Island. Eventually I picked up the book that Mr Lipton had given me, I do not remember leaving it on the couch, yet there it was right beside where the Butler had been sitting. I read the spine;

'J.Wilkes, Demonology- the history of Britain's supernatural beings'

J Wilkes, is that James who I had tea with? It couldn't be. No, this book was written in 1735, one hundred and fifty years ago. An ancestor I suppose. It had to be. On the third page there was a short forward.

'All you seek can be found thriving in the dark, but in the sun they draw you to them."

The words triggered a part of my brain that I had been trying to ignore. Anna's face once more appeared in my mind. The pages had been well fingered, old grease stained every page. Small annotations had been made beside different monsters as if someone had been studying them. I flicked through the pages once by one, glancing only at the names of the creatures.

Werewolf, Vampyr, Fae, Black dogs, Dwarves, Elves, Ghosts, Boggarts, Dragons in the Highlands, Ogre's and more that I had never thought of. Close to the back the pages had been folded down haphazardly.

'The Siren- A water Demon'

The picture drawn, an etching from a long time ago, it was teeth long and sharp, a tail that was long and wrapped around its prey to hold it tight. Usually grey skinned with pale eyes that held the gaze of any one who looked at them. A song so beautiful it ensnared any man who heard it.

My heart felt heavy as I read on.

'Some variants may use a venom-like substance which can be passed through saliva into the bloodstream, rendering their victim unable to move and blurr the mind. Each man subdued by the variant is then taken through a sexual ritual binding the two together. The only way to separate the bond is for one the pair to die.'

I pushed the book onto a side table and breathed out. Flashes of memory coming back to me. I was at the window swiftly, moving without knowing. From there I could see the tower, dark against the skyline. Part of my heart began to break. Anna broke me, more than I could ever have known. Could she really be a Siren? What else is being hidden from me? What else are they lying about to me?

I stood there until I could stand no longer.

08/10/1885

It has been days and I can't find anything in this damn cottage.
Books here are useless. She's singing.

Why won't she stop singing?

I knew what she did to me. They've all lied to me. Every one of them.

Cassandra lied to me. How could she do that to me?

I should leave.

How do I leave

Stop singing.

Please stop singing.

Siren's call, calling to me. Every syllable reaches out to me.

Stop it.

Stop the singing.

Please

Stop.

10/10/1885

I think something else is afoot here.

Perhaps I should take some time away from here.

She still sings, the song is calling to me. My name in every word she sings.

How do I stop it?

The book, the words - Death is the only way. My gun.

A gun kept here inside the walls of the cottage. My clothes telling me where to find it, on a note, given by a friend? Perhaps, or it could have been the horses. I had been standing with the horses. I have been holding the gun in my hands every day.

They want me to work, to help the builders. Leaving the cottage. I can't do that. I try, I can get now one foot over the threshold but that singing. It frightens me. I retreat to my walls.

How do I carry on? I cannot work with her calling out to me. I hear her now even in my sleep.

I will do it now, inside this room. If I went outside to her now she would have me. Whole and complete.

The gun is loaded.
I'll go now, the house is quiet and everyone is asleep. The key is in my pocket, it opens every door.

Here at the first door, what could she be hiding? The key opened it easily and I slid inside. All around me are statues, marbled? no , just polished. They aren't human. One has tails, this one has horns. What are these? No answers there, the second door, that must help me. Mirrors? Tall ones, small ones, free standing and wall mounted. All around me mirrors. The room goes on far longer than it should be able to and all of it mirrors. No windows I can see but there is a light bouncing between the mirrors.
My head began to spin. Too many versions of myself facing back at me. The entrance hall is dark. I'll go through the door below the staircase. In the day it leads to the kitchens. There, another door. I tried it locked, but not for long.

It is dark, too dark. The darkness beacons me to come to it. I can hear it growling.
The gun is in my hand, I hear it.

The Portsmouth Times & Navel Gazette

After a week of non stop operatic songs coming from the Umbra Island, the Duchess Whetton has announced the unfortunate death of her Aunt, Lady Anna.

The seventy two year old sister of Mr Whetton, the Duchess' father, had suffered with a brain shrinking disability for over thirty years, becoming a recluse within the old mansion's walls.

Sources believe the recent renovations at the mansion became too much for the poor woman, who was standing at her window singing her beloved arias from the old operas.

It has been told to us that she refused to eat and had become more and more violent towards the family and household staff, after a home invasion a few weeks ago. Lady Anna threw herself from the fourth floor window, landing somewhat ironically on the family graveyard site. Some may say it was an apt place for her to take her final breath.

It is said that Queen Victoria has sent a gift of condolences of a marble coffin for the aged woman who once had been a friend of the royal court. The two women had lept a written correspondence since the Queen's childhood. Her Majesty is said to be releasing a statement detailing her bereavement at the loss of her friend later this week. The pair had met as children and Lady Anna had been one of the few children allowed in the young Queen's presence;

bonding them both in a unique relationship. Lady Anna was known within the Queen's court as a friend and confident for many years.

Rumours of a funeral tomb for Lady Anna is said to have been started in what was her favourite part of the Island. It is unknown how long the tomb will take to be erected.

The people of Portsmouth, though happy to hear the end of the singing, are saddened by the news of her passing.

Here at the Portsmouth times and Navel Gazette we wish to send our own condolences to the Duchess and Mr Whetton on their unfortunate loss.

14/10/1885

The house is oddly quiet now Anna is gone. Now we are without it, I miss the sound of her voice. Still, I no longer feel the fear I did a week ago. My whole body feels lighter somehow. My mind is clearer in a way it hasn't been since I got to this Island. I knew it the moment she was gone; I felt it. I had the gun in my hand, unsure if I was going to brave the walk to her or take myself out of the equation, then it was all gone. In my mind I saw her falling as if I was looking through her eyes until a second before she hit the ground. At last I feel free to wander as I please with no fear of being hurt. Everyday I spend more time with Cassandra and my feelings for her are growing every stronger. It is all I can do to stop myself from kissing her each time we are together. Even Charles has begun to lighten to my presence. In point of fact I have never felt more part of a family as I do now.

Don't fear, I put the gin away. I do not need it now.

Cassandra stayed true to her word and though we mourn the loss of Anna, the tailor came to the house. He fitted both myself and Charles for new suits. I haven't been taken care of so wonderfully since I was a teenager and my father was trying to show me off to his friends. Life here could be so much fun, I can tell that much. So long, of course, if we continue to get along as famously as we have been.

A spot of tea is exactly what the doctor ordered. A good spot of tea.

Charles will have to go, he cannot stay here if I want her. A Duchess can not have two husbands. It must look as accidental as I can make it. The building work could be perfect. Or Beleadoner, it grows on the east side. How sad that he died of a broken heart , after his sister's death. What a shame for *him*. We would all be sad.

I find all our activities to be most wonderful. Cassandra and myself. It is the grandest of times when we are together. Always laughing and enjoying our days.

Especially when

18/10/1885

A cloud lifted yesterday. I couldn't tell you exactly what happened, there is still something missing. The last few entries in this journal are confusing to me. I do not think I wrote them, but the penmanship is a perfect match to my own.

I woke up this morning in the library at the house, slumped over the desk. This journal was tucked below the papers I had been studying. Everything feels strange to me. As if I'm not really here, like my mind is projecting me into the house. Each step I take feels too soft, like I hold no weight or traction within the space. Time is moving slower for me almost. I watch the people around me moving about in their normal duties, all unaware of my thoughts. The building work in the ballroom was close to finishing and the entrance hall had been completed with new carpets and the curtains replaced with bright mint green velvet. I am sure it all has its own special names, mostly that side of things have been left to Cassandra and the contractor.

Because of this being done, I was able to finish my work early today so I have sneaked back to the cottage. I need to mourn in my own way. Part of me wished I could have had more time with Anna. Had the opportunity to get more acquainted with her in a more personal way. Perhaps without the rest of the family around. Still, perhaps it has been for the best that we did not. If I am to believe the Duchess then Anna had been ill much like my own aunt. I should contact the home she resides in, check if my aunt is still, well I assume she is alive as I am still paying for her keep. I will write to them this evening. It may be pertinent to put a plan in place for her; encase I am ever unable to provide payment for her care. Excuse me, I have come off topic.

The tomb erected for Anna is not new as the papers would have you believe. The thing looks almost ancient now. With ivy and moss growing wild over it and dead autumn leaves dusting the ground outside it. Mr Litpon enjoyed telling me about it. The walls are at least four foot deep on each side with a layer of iron plating covering the walls, floor and ceiling on the inside. In the middle stands a large sarcophagus type coffin waiting to hold her body forever. I do not understand the odd use of Egyptian mythology. It was often appearing around the Island when it had no right to be there.

Across the Island there are three other tombs the same as this one. . According to the paperwork I found one holds Cassandra's parents, one is earmarked for the Duchess herself and the other, the largest of the four, had been earmarked for staff who die in service of the family. I couldn't understand how someone who had erected them over one hundred years ago could have known the names of the current family. I remembered this morning about the first conversation I had at the library in London. The curse. The Whetton family curse.

There was a rumour surrounding their banishment to the Island. People spoke of a dark night, strange creatures running the streets of London. The Whetton family had been unfortunate victims. Then a hunt had begun, some say witches had been involved, or that it was a witch hunt, stories differed by who had written them. Not much else was known, or told to me about what truly happened to them. I can't help thinking that the Duke, his wife and daughter are the only ones that have ever been this family.

I know there is a way to find out more about it. There has to be. I have taken many books from the library back to my cottage, amongst them I have secreted paperwork from the family's archives for the past hundred years. There must be a clue in them. There is not nearly enough time for me to read it all yet. An opportunity could be found if I stay back from the funeral. No, that is no good at all. Cassandra has kept such a tight hold on me the last few days. Bedtime is my only solace from any company. Although I am sure they have posted someone to keep a watch on my cottage at night.

Wait!

I apologise, I remembered something, the walls in this room. They are not as they seem. When I was having tea with James and Amelia they told me to watch the walls. Till now I couldn't make out what they had meant, now I do. The wall around the fireplace in my room has no alcoves. The other rooms do. I do not have time to do it tonight, the sun is already coming up in the east. I shall endeavour to finish my work early tomorrow. I will take some tools from the workers. It will not take long, I think anyway. Just a moment ao I tapped on the wall, it is most definitely hollow. The true thickness of the wall may be more than I bargain for. It could take some time to get through it.

I should not write my plans down here. Words have not been my own recently. Anyone who reads this should take heed of all that happens to me. It could have been anyone. I know they had removed it from this cottage, for I never would and still it was with me in the library.

Something is wrong here.

It is Tuesday.

Today is Anna's funeral. I have thus far been unable to do anything with the bedroom walls. Most of yesterday was spent with Cassandra. I cannot tell you if I stay with her by my own mind or by hers. When I am with her all I can think about is her, she consumes all of me. I want to walk away, leave it all and then I see her and my whole body wants her, to hold her, feel her, have her. I have never felt this way about anyone, not this strongly.

On my arrival to the house this morning, I was greeted by voices in the parlour. I pushed myself up against the door to listen.

"If you want him, let me go!" He shouted.

"It isn't time." She replied.

"I am finished with this ruse. Tell me the truth, why is he so different from the rest of us?"

A moment of silence, I could hear Charles moving around the room.

"I feel, Charles; I feel things that I have never felt and I feel it for him."

"You are incapable of love. You are still just a petulant child. You always have been so spoiled by everyone around you."

He moved again and the conversation muffled. Cassandra screamed. Her cry ripped through my chest. I had to kick the door several times, finally breaking the lock from the wood. Inside Cassandra was on the ground, Charles standing over her, holding one of her wrists. Her face was wet with tears, a line of blood dripped from her mouth.

"Step away Mr Whetton." I spoke as sternly as I could, squaring my shoulders and jaw. The older man did the same, forcefully shoving

Cassandra away from him, her shoulder hit into a side table as she fell. He stood to his full height and stomped across the room, stopping mere inches away from me. My chest shook slightly, I tried to keep my composure, straightening my back further to lessen the height difference. His dark eyes bore into mine.

"You can have her, but take heed of the darkness, Mr Whitman." The words came out with a broken voice. I swallowed though my mouth was dry., turned slightly and walked past him, my shoulder nudging him as I went.

I dropped down next to the Duchess, pulling her close to me, making sure not to pull her too quickly. My hand cradled her head. I turned back to Charles. He was watching Cassandra's hand move to hold onto my shirt, a tear fell from his eye and his fingers twitched. He sighed when we made eye contact then left the room.

"Are you okay, Your Grace?" I asked, holding her cheek. She nodded.

"More shock than anything else." Cassandra tried to laugh. I used my thumb to wipe the blood from her chin.

"You must send him away, Cassandra!" I pleaded with her.

"Not yet, I cannot, he is grieving his sister."

I could not help the way my face fell.

"What's wrong?" She asked me.

"I may only be your lawyer, an employee or a conquest, but Cassandra please do not lie to me. I know he is not your father."

I saw how her eyes widened at my words, she opened her mouth to talk. As she often did but no words came out. My eyes closed.

"Okay, Your Grace, Duchess, let's get you cleaned up ." She held onto my arms and I lifted her up to her feet.

I stayed with her all day. We walked in the gardens, she showed me the hidden swing she played on as a child. The rope had broken a long time ago. I promised to fix it one day. We sat down together on the grass. Somehow daisies were still blooming, in the October chill. Cassandra started using them to make chains. A bruise had risen up on the side of her face, covering the bottom half of her jaw. At times I found myself staring at her. I had almost forgotten how her eyes were almost colourless. In the autumnal sunlight they were full of colour, blue, purple, green, gold, so many different reflections in them. A piece of her hair had fallen out of place during the altercation, it was now lying down the side of her face, curling just above her jaw. I do not suppose I have ever studied a person's face in such detail as I have with hers. Perhaps once as a child when my parents had taken me to the circus. There had been a woman whose whole body was covered in tattoos. I could not help but stare at the way the pictures wrapped around her curves. The simple fact of almost all of her flesh being on show probably did not help the matter to my twelve year old eyes. That is all beside the point.

"Tell me more about your family, Horetio?" Cassandra asked. I could not answer at first. My mind was caught in the memory of the circus. She stroked the back of my hand to gain my attention.

"I do not remember much of my mother, she died when I was nine. I remember her warmth, she was never too busy for me or my sister."

"Sister? I didn't know you had a sister. I would love to meet her."

That sentence caught my breath and held onto it for a moment.

"She would have been fond you, I think." I played with the grass in front of my crossed legs. Cassandra stayed quiet, "She died along with my mother."

"What happened to them?" The sun burnt my eyes through the closed lids.

"It's my...I was at school, a boarding school in the North. I was having some trouble with a few of the lads there. Older boys. We were on the running team together; they didn't like me very much. It doesn't matter really, just that it took my father away from the house. The head teacher called for him.

He left my mother and sister at home alone. Father had recently fired a man from our service. The police say he came back and he, he killed them. Catherine was only five years old and he. It isn't fair. I know my father blamed me for it. If he had still been at home instead of with me..." I closed my eyes tight. Her hand squeezed my shoulder.

"I am so sorry, Horatio. I should never have asked." she said.

"No, it is okay, Cassandra. You should know everything about me. I want my future and my past to be yours." I looked into her eyes and she looked into mine.

"You do?"

"If you want it, then yes, it is yours. Before you make that choice you should know everything about me. I want you to be fully aware of who I am." My words were truthful yet tactful. My heart spoke though my mind twisted the words to fit my purpose. I hoped she would reciprocate the sentiment.

"I agree full disclosure on all our secrets is best. Still shall we allow our bedlam to come out slowly and not all in one go?" She giggled.

"All right, slowly." I agreed, a smile on my face.

She ran her hand down my arm onto my hand. I turned my hand so hers rested in my palm, her skin so cold. It was always cold, even when sitting beside a fire her fingers were like ice in mine. For what felt like hours we sat this way, yet no time had passed at all.

"Do you miss London?" She asked.

I laughed, I suppose in a way I did. Not the city so much, I missed the friends I had made. The evenings were spent drinking with the boys from university. Mrs Hobbs and the way she would fuss about me. She was more than just a landlady to me; an old family friend really.

I couldn't tell you how I knew her for sure, I believe I met her when I was a child.

Of course the quick pace of everything always made me feel uncomfortable so I was pleased to be away from that. People in London often had no regard for anyone else on the streets. All rushing about, bumping and knocking into each other without a thought to apologise. The Island was far better and less crowded.

When I finished replying to her I had talked myself round in circles about the whole situation. Cassandra stayed quiet throughout my babbling, only nodding at the appropriate times. I stopped talking, pressing my lips together. It was Cassandra's turn to laugh at me.

"You are so stoic, Mr Whitman. Tell me, do you ever relax?"

"I try to, in my own way. Reading for one."

"Old dusty books from an old dusty library? I'm not sure how my grandfather's ancient texts could relax anyone." She was laughing again.

"Well I enjoy more new authors, recent books. Why are you laughing, Your Grace? It is a common past time" Especially for your sex." I pleaded.

"Oh, because I am a woman I should be wilting in a dark corner; reading sonnets from Shakespere or would you prefer I embroidered flowers on material that will be forgotten in an attic? Is that what you look for in a woman, sir? A flower so delicate, she might fall apart with your strong touch?"

"Quite the opposite, My Duchess. Women that fragile have their place in the world I am sure, and the men who want for them are many. For me, however, it would be an unfulfilled life. I would be a much happier man with a woman who could challenge me and my beliefs. For a wife I want a woman who is as willing to berate me as she is to praise me." I had tilted my head away from her, looking out over the gardens, "My mother would challenge my father like no other. Not even his peers could put him in his place; and yet, I never saw anyone please him the way she did. I don't, I could not settle for anything less than that in a relationship." Her eyes were on me, I could feel them.

I glanced at her without moving my head, the emotion on her face was unreadable at that angle.

"You are different from other men." She said flatly. I shook my head.

"No, not really. I don't think men will want to be so plain in their views on a woman's role in the future. Who knows what it really holds for that side of things, but I am not so different from other men. I still want a good woman beside me, a good income and a happy life."

Cassandra shifted her dress around herself and slid closer to me. Her body was so close to mine I could see her pulse pumping beneath the skin on her neck. The scent of lavender weaker outside drifted over me once again. I tasted her before her lips reached mine. My eyes closed the instant we touched. A desire filled me. Nothing else mattered to me at that moment. Not the birds in the trees or the wind that blew around us. For my mind all there could be was Cassandra. My hand reached up around her face, entangling into her red hair. I lifted her body onto my lap, holding her close to me with my other hand. The wanting was matched in her, clear by her actions. Both her hands held me tightly. Small mews came from her throat that spurred me on.

As gently as my rushing mind would allow me I flipped us round so her back was against the grass. Without breaking our kiss she helped to push my coat off my shoulders. I was unaware of where it fell. My hand reached down, running over her corseted waist, past her hips and slowly began to pull her skirts up. With every inch it moved I waited for her cue to stop. Her cold flesh rubbed against my fingertips. She felt good. I pulled back, my chest heaving, trying to catch my breath. Our eyes met.

"Are you sure about this? We do not have to do anything?" I whispered. Cassandra looked at me, once again I couldn't decipher the emotion in her eyes. Her tongue swept across her lips.

"I..." She began but didn't finish.

"God I do not want to, but perhaps we should wait." I suggested moving myself away from her. With a nod she also sat up. The two of us sat in silence for a short while; both catching our breaths. I closed my eyes and concentrated on calming my body as much as my mind.

"We should return to the house, the company there may keep our minds on a safer path." She suggested. As we stood she handed me my coat, then took my arm to walk back to the house. A million questions were rushing around my head, all fighting to get out and be asked. My mouth would not allow a single one to be voiced. The Duchess too stayed quiet, while we walked.

We did little else over lunch, the cook made us a selection of bread and meats and fruits. In an attempt to make fun of our conversation she pulled a book from the library, sitting in the window seat. I pretended to read as well though I spent more time watching her than paying attention to the words. I watched how her neck curved so perfectly to rest her head against the window pain.

Around five o'clock Mr Lipton entered the room, he told us that Mr Whetton was waiting by the entrance and wished to speak to me. I puffed myself out, straightened my clothing, nodded to Cassandra and followed the butler out to the entrance hall.

"Mr Whitman, there is little to say on this day. I will be staying on the eastern shore line, in the guest cottage for the next few weeks. I feel it is best for us all."

"Mr Whetton, I do not pretend to understand all that happens on this Island. Many days I am unsure if what I see is truly possible. Yet there is never a time that it is acceptable to hurt a person in your care." I put as much conviction into my words as I could. Charles looked at me, his eyes blank of emotion.

"You would be careful to see who owns who in this house. Be warned, Mr Whitman, the walls here are not all in place as they seem. Be sure to care for my daughter, she is not safe without me here. Should you return to your cottage the kitchen holds a secret amongst the china. It will help you understand."

We simply looked at each other. He nodded, turned and left. I told Mr Lipton to send Lilly down to Charles' cottage along with food and supplies for about a week. I explained it would be right for Mr Whetton to have at least the maid working there. He agreed and sent the girl on her way. She smiled at me with sad eyes as she went.

I said goodnight to Cassandra around nine in the evening after supper and made my way back to my own cottage. I wrote a quick note detailing Charles' information on my current home, pinned it to the kitchen door and forced myself to sleep.

Today I have awoken solemnly, a sadness waving over me that I did not anticipate feeling. All morning members of the royal family and parliament joined the toffs of high society filtering on to the Island. Each of them acted like they had been personal friends with Anna. Sickening. Several socialites from France had also come across to the Island. An outsider might have thought the family were holding a grand celebration not a funeral.

I saw a priest walk up the long path from the dock to the house. Even from my distance I spotted the hesitations in every step the holy man took. It was clear from my first day that religion was scarcely remembered or cared for by the Island residents.

Charles had been hanging around the house, everyone pretending nothing had happened the day before. I was unsurprised by it. Cassandra had used makeup to cover the bruise by her lip. What did surprise me was how easily she ignored yesterday. Chatting with Charles as if no angered words had passed between them. Part of me boiled at the thought of him standing anywhere close to her. Cassandra should be on my arm not his. Despite my money and status from my father to the world I am nothing more than a lawyer, an employee of the Duchess. I will walk amongst the procession in my proper place.

The day threatened a rainfall with grey clouds overhead. Fitting weather for the sadness of the day in my opinion. My mother and sister's funeral was the same, at least from what I can remember of it. Father had insisted I attend. All around me that day people cried and told me how sorry they were. It was all false. Just like this one, those that attend are there to be seen by everyone else. Honestly I would be happier if only my true family attended mine. I suspect in actual fact I would have no one attend with my aunt being the way she is.

The ceremony for Anna was as any other with the priest reading from the bible. His eyes often flicking to and from Cassandra, sweat beading on his forehead in the cold chapel. He led us all silently to the tomb where Mr Lipton, Charles and four other men carried the marbled coffin down the stone steps. We heard the iron sarcophagus lid slide heavy into place. Five men came back up. I asked Mrs Lipton where the last man was. She told me that it was tradition for one man to stay behind for the first night; a way of keeping the spirit company before it passes over. I can't say I believe him at all, it had been over a week since her death, surely her spirit would have already passed on to whatever new land it was intended for days ago. I kept my misgivings to myself, lingering for just long enough behind the others to see the heavy iron door pushed into place and sealed.

I spent little time at the wake, staying long enough for one beverage before returning to my cottage. I dropped my coat and tie on the stand by the door, disregarded my shoes not far from that. My chest still felt tight when I breathed heavily so I stood still before the welsh dresser in the kitchen. The words Charles had said to me in my head, taunting me.

Inside me a spark burst into a flame. I pushed the plates away letting them smash on the floor. Small tea cups followed, until my feet were surrounded. Nothing was there, not obvious to me. My fingers ran over the wood feeling every bump and valley. On the top shelf the wood moved, under the pressure from my hand. A block slid out of place. It had been hollowed out. Inside was a folded slip of paper and an iron key. The paper had a sketch of the fireplace upstairs with an arrow pointing to the mantle. I turned on the spot, slamming my foot down on the broken china. Expletives left my mouth as I tried to hop over the mess, landing on the now wounded foot, slipping on my own blood and sliding into the door frame, knocking my shoulder. I growled, pushing myself back up, limping into the living room.

How many more injuries am I to endure? The scar on my hand still pained me from time to time. My fingertips still showed the heat damage from the stables fire as well. I pulled off my sock to reveal the shard of china sticking out of my instep. Lips open, bearing my clenched teeth I pulled it from my skin.
"Wonderful!" I grumbled, wrapping the cotton cloth from the table around my foot.

I was exhausted. I am exhausted. I think I shall go to bed now.

21/10/1885

I did not sleep. It is funny what exhaustion really does to a person. This morning I watched as the funeral guests filtered back to the boats just as they had arrived. All going back to their perfect unassuming lives. I laughed to myself, thinking how they must have been longing for a scandal to be revealed. Some dirty secret to be let out amongst the gathered. They will have learnt, as I have, the walls here do not talk unless you have a key. A key I know have in my possession. I have been itching to use it, to open the wall and see what lies behind it just waiting for me.

Unfortunately I have to wait as Cassaandra requested my presence during the day. She is inspecting the almost completed work in the ballroom. Frankly the work that had been done was magnificent in my opinion. The carved walls and ceilings had been restored with fine precision. Vibrant new drapes had been hanged at the patio doors and windows. The staircase that led to Cassandra's corridore was now laid with an olive green runner and curved the length of the room as it descended. New lights had been wired into every nook of the ceiling, they tell me it will give the illusion of starlights in a night sky. The flooring had been restored to its glory with a lot of varnish and hard work. The Duchess was delighted with all of it. She spun around in the middle of the room then pulled me into the spin. I had not seen her this happy at all since my arrival. The smile on her face was divine in its beauty. It was easy for me to get swept up into her infectious happiness. She dismissed the contractor and his men, agreeing with them that work would begin again on the rest of the house after the ball. We sat in the room together on the floor. Cassandra laid back, looking up at the painting above us.

"Horatio?"

"Yes?" I laid back beside her.

"Are you looking to marry a woman one day?" She kept her eyes trained on the ceiling.

"I um, yes I suppose, if the right woman were to agree to it." I said.

"Do you think you have met that woman already?" Her voice trembles slightly.

"Perhaps, though I believe there is more for us to know about each other before I could trust her heart in my hands." I was not lying, a part of me had fallen for the Duchess, her scent haunted my mind and still I had so many unanswered questions. The way my mind felt altered in some way. Days missing from my memory. Moments that felt like dream and reality all at once.

Anna, still my biggest question is Anna. Is the book right? Is that why she is entombed in iron? So many questions, but how do I ask them? How do I ask her any of it?

"And if that woman was to give you her heart willingly, would you take it?" Her eyes had pulled her head to face me, her fingers playing with mine.

"I would ask for more time, if the woman truly loved me she would understand that I needed more time; for my mind to catch up with my heart." I closed my eyes, hardly wanting to know her answer. No answer came verbally. My fingers were left cold, and the sweep of her dress echoed in the empty space beside me. I was left alone with the ticking of the grand clock behind me.

"More time." I said to myself.

I did not linger for long in the ballroom. Instead I forced my body to get up and come back to the cottage. Stepping through the door I knew something was wrong. Objects had been moved, knocked to the ground. I followed the path, against my instincts up to the stairs. The fire poker was solid and heavy in my hand. I tried to keep my footsteps quiet on my ascent. My mouth was drying out. The door to my bedroom was directly on the top step of the stairs. The closer I got the more the smell filled me, offended me. The wooden door was hot to touch, still I pushed it open. White flames flickered around the fireplace. Every hair on my body stood on end. Two cold eyes looked at me, I knew him. They were all that I had seen of him that day. The flames turned away from the wall, slowly coming towards me.

"Marcoff?" his name came out whispered. The flames burst, burning brighter. "Marcoff, stop!" I tried to command whatever entity this was. It came closer, the flames heating my skin. I had backed to the wall. The white flames began to die down, every nerve in my body screamed at me. Gradually Marcoff's human form could be seen. At last I looked upon the full face of my driver on the first day I came to the Island.

"Why are you here?" I asked.

His hand pointed past me, beyond me to the house, before turning back to the fireplace.

"The stables, that was you wasn't it?" Marcoff's eyes blinked, can a ghost cry? He turned, moving to the bed, holding his glowing hand over the demonology book. The pages began flipping by themselves, finally settling on a page. Holding my breath I moved beside him.

"A Spectre of unfulfilled destiny. Is that what you are?" I understood what it meant. Marcoff should never have died when he did, there were still things in this place for him to do.

"It wasn't highwaymen that killed you, was it?"

Marcoff shook his head.

"What are they?" I asked. He turned again all but gliding back to the wall. "Of course." I followed his path, pulling the key and sketch from my waistcoat pocket. My mind tried to ignore that I was standing beside a ghost.

The drawing pointed to the wooden mantle. Just as I had done with the welsh dresser in the kitchen I ran my fingers over it. A space in front of the mirror, it slipped open revealing a keyhole. With a glance back at Marcoff I put the key inside and turned it. Cogs turned behind the wall and with a puff of dust it opened. The wall had separated from the mantle. Damp air momentarily swept away the burning scent of the ghost behind me.

I pulled the wall open further, finally seeing what I had been longing for. Answers in the form of books, journals written by four men. The most recent held twelve journals all together, with the last one ending not too long ago.

Each of them started the same way.

The Wilkes firm has sent me here to ensure the client's finances are correct.

History repeating itself over and over. I began to pull the journals out, moving about the room in almost a trance. By the time I had finished and looked up again Marcoff and his white flames were gone.

I woke up this morning still leaning against the headboard of my bed. After documenting my day last night I delved in the journals. The first one I had started I've yet to find a name. Thinking about it, I have not yet formally introduced myself to you. I am Horetio Whitman, lawyer and heir to moderate estate. I will go back and write my name on the inside cover of this book. I wonder if I would make much sense to anyone reading my scribbles. I doubt they would make any at all unless you were living these events yourself. The same could be said for the one I read now, it could be verbatim my own with the beginning of the story. This man was older than my twenty-eight years, he was already into his thirties upon his arrival. He arrived early in the morning and came straight to the cottage. As I read each page caused a knot in my stomach to grow. There were moments I had thought the bile inside me would bubble up too high for me to keep it down.

I am not sure when I fell asleep, but both my candles had burnt down to nothing and I was left with a crick in my neck. I blinked away the dreariness, stretched my neck side to side. I couldn't tell you why, something moved my hands without my prior consent, flipping the journal to one of the last pages. The words on the page seared into my mind. I shall repeat them here.

'The Duchess, no more a witch than I - in point of fact she is immortal. Her parents are to blame. The Egyption tomb was not theirs to open, yet they did it. Rinsworth's journal explains it fully.
The woman feels nothing, no pain, no hunger, no cold, no love.'
She takes the husbands and lives their life time. I am next. I cannot say no to her now. I am entirely hers. Her magic is tied to this house.

My shoulders dropped. Is this real? I knew I was wanted at the house today. This new knowledge was swimming through my mind bringing every memory of my time with Cassandra into a new light. Did I truly feel anything for her? Is it all a lie? There was no time to think about it. Cassandra was wanting to go through arrangements for the ball. I assumed she still wanted to. After our strained conversation yesterday I couldn't be sure if that was still the case today.

With shaky legs I changed my shirt and waistcoat before heading off to the house. I caught sight of Charles as he was walking toward the house. He nodded his head once in my direction. I nodded back. Connections in my brain coming together in my mind.

"Mr Whitman." His voice broke my thoughts.

"Good morning, Mr Whetton." I replied.

"I want you to be aware first. I will be leaving the Island for a while." Charles said.

"In the current circumstances that is probably advisable. How long will you be travelling away?"

"Two weeks, to start with. I will miss the Duchess' ball, however I expect you will assure her protection and enjoyment." He was looking toward the burnt stables instead of me. I followed his eyeline, watching the house staff milling around. Charles flicked his eyes back to me briefly. "Be cautious of her guests, they will not be what you expect. You have found the journals I see. Read every word, it may save your soul."

"Mr Whetton, if you truly do love her how can you hurt her?" I asked.

Charles' eyes looked down at me, creases evident around them and his mouth turned down.

"Love is different for us all. It runs so closely in parallel to hate. You will understand in time." I wanted to continue our conversation, get him to tell me everything he knows. I was not given that chance as Charles stormed away from me with an unnatural speed in my own opinion. I stayed in my place for a while, my feet unable to move as my mind raced with thoughts. Could any of this be real? Have I really stumbled into a work of immortality and magic? It was a book that came to life. A Jules Vern perhaps. If it is true and Charles first met the Duchess as a young man, how can she still be so youthful herself? Immortality, I could not, will not believe it. Still, the way I have felt, surely if it was magic I would be wholeheartedly within it. There would be no chance of my questioning whether my feelings were true or not. The Charles that had once written the words in the journal seemed so far from the man I know now. Was there a way to really understand all of this? Are the journals enough or is there something else I could find? Behind one of the locked doors perhaps. I cannot simply ask Cassandra outright. If any of it is untrue my strange accusations could ruin everything I have here.

A large crow flew past me. Crows seemed to be everywhere here. A murder of crows in every direction. Large black birds that stalked the grounds, sitting on the roofs of each building. Their caws even haunt my dreams at night. The wing of this one almost clipped my face, and the bird landed on the grass beside me. Our eyes met, brown to obsidian. Of course, even to me, it is crazy to think that the bird had any thoughts on my situation. I still wondered what his answer would be. His eyes spoke to me, calmed me somehow. I have to be sure, everything must be completely straight in my mind. Standing there silently communicating with a crow I made a choice. I will go on as if I know nothing more than I did a week ago. I will read every journal in the cottage, document what I can in this one and gather as much information as I can.

Cassandra met me at the entrance to the house. She was smiling, showing no care for our previous meeting.
"My lawyer! Excellent, come I am about to speak with Mrs Lipton. You should accompany me. The old woman will need the reassurance that we are not overspending on my little party." She was giggling between her words. Her happiness was already infecting me. It was easy to get carried away with it and I did. She grabbed my hand, pulling me into the kitchen where the housekeeper was already waiting with a pot of tea.

The three of us chatted for around two hours, going over the decorations, food and music. The Duchess had been insistent on a full orchestra, she even knew the exact group she wanted. Mrs Lipton appeared to be happy with the choice. I had not heard of them myself.
"Will they be available, so quickly? It is short notice." I asked. Both women laughed.
"Of course, they always come to our celebrations. They would do anything for our Duchess." Mrs Lipton answered. The housekeeper was adamant that we would need at least ten chefs for food preparations. I was reluctant but outvoted.

All together the ball was planned to cost around six hundred pounds. The Duchess hardly cared about the numbers, which both annoyed and delighted me.

After the meeting with the women I was taken for a final fitting for my new suit. It was going to be snug but it felt wonderful. I had renewed my excitement for the evening, all my reservations being pushed away. It is an odd feeling for me, I do not know how to explain it to you. I will try.

When I am with Cassandra I feel safe, at peace. It is as though all my worries about this Island and its inhabitants disappear from my mind almost entirely. Unfortunately or fortunately, depending on your view on the matters. When I return to the cottage it all goes away. My chest tightens and I fear her. I honestly do fear her. I fear the whole house. As I read these journals, my entire body screams at me to pack my bags and leave. The thought of doing that makes me anxious. Could I do that? They would find me wouldn't they? Able to leave the Island or not. No, Horetio stay on track.

By the time I had returned to my small sanctuary I had convinced myself that the ball was the most important night of our lives. The guest list had been left out on the table so I sneaked a look at it. I had been expecting to see the names of London's society; not one. I did not recognise many of them at all. The Honourable twins Mia and Micheal of France.

Baroness Montreal of Berlin

Countess Bathory

Vlad, a Count from Romania

A Holy man from Russia

Several American women from a small town. I couldn't understand why there was such a strange list of people. I wondered if I could find out who they were beforehand. One person would be able to help me.

I called for Lilly the maid, it was easy given the mess in the kitchen, I had yet to clean up. When she came in I waited, allowing her to do the work she was expecting to do. My palms were wet with sweat when she eventually came back to the living room.

"Lilly, please sit, have a cup of tea with me?" I asked.

She looked around the room, shuffled her dress and sat on the edge of the chair. Her hands held in her lap.

"I know you are uncomfortable with these conversations. I do need you to help me as much as you can. Please can you tell me who the Duchess' guests are?" I said.

"Mr Whitman, please, they are all friends of the Duchess. People she has known for many years. They call themselves the enlightened. A society almost impossible to join. I can not say much else as I do not know more. You must be cautious though when you are amongst them."

I was quiet, looking at her. Her head lowered slightly, eyes shifting back forth to the door. She flicked her tongue out, wetting her lips before drawing the bottom one momentarily between her teeth. The action did something to me, inside. A feeling only those who enjoy her gender could understand. I ignored it.

"Lilly, is any of this real? Do I really have feelings for her?" I poured out a cup of tea from the teapot as I spoke.

"I could not tell you sir. Do you think about her when you are alone?" she asked.

My breath came out long and drawn out.

"I do but I think of others as well." I said.

"You do?" Her eyes shot to mine.

"Mhm yes. It is odd, in the immediate hours after leaving her I can think only of her face. Yet a different face calls to me in the dead of night." Confessing to Lilly was a confession to myself. I had been attempting to keep this attraction unspoken. The hope that history would not repeat itself.

Lilly's eyes widened at the words that came from me, a smile pulling at her lips. In a whisper she told me of her feelings for me. I dropped to my knees in front of her, placing my hands on hers.

"What do I do, Lilly? I am so confused about this all. Everyone here seems one way then changes the next day. I have been led to believe your father is an evil man who beats women, yet he has shown his love for you, and been a man of a magnanimous nature when we are alone. He has left his entire fortune to you. Upon his death you become a rich woman with a title. Still I am entranced by the Duchess as well. Everything on this island seems to lead back to you or her."

One hand slid out from under mine., cupped my face and made me look up to her. Silently she bent down and kissed me. This kiss was different to any the Duchess and I had shared. This was soft, so delicate I hardly felt it. My body melted, all my muscles relaxing into her touch. I kept my eyes closed when she pulled away.

"Lilly." I whispered her name, too scared to talk out loud. We stayed that way for a few minutes, it was not long enough for me.

"I should go." Her own voice was barely louder than mine was.

"I wish you would stay." I was all but begging her. It felt like begging with my knees on the ground. She shook her head and I felt the moment shatter.

"I have work at the house. I should get back."

My body dropped backwards, making room for her to stand. This could not be the way this would end. I had hidden this want for so long, I could not allow it to end now. I jumped to my feet, climbed over the couch, reaching for her. My hand slid around her waist, the hard boning of her corset stiff under my fingers.

"Please, Lilly, stay for a moment longer." I pulled her closer to me, pressing out bodies together. Her breath swept over me.

"Sir, I..." I put my head to hers, a long breath fell out of my mouth.

"Be careful, Lilly, you are always in danger in that house."

With a small curtsey Lilly slid herself through the front door. I shut it behind her and darted upstairs to my bedroom window to watch her return to the house.

What is happening to me? Why do I feel like this? My body was on fire with desire for two women.

"I know I should leave her be, but what if we were able to get away?" I spoke to the spectre beside me. Marcoff turned his head to the books on my bed, pointed to one of the older journals. This ghost was persistent, desperate for me to read the story of dead men.

I have tried to keep myself away from both Lilly and Cassandra over the last few days. Reading the journals when I could, helping to organise the newly hired staff, readying them for the ball. Anything to keep myself busy and unavailable.

You probably think I am mad, but I think I have finally sorted a plan. I have Charles' will with a bag of things ready to go. I have also managed to steal away three dresses from Cassandra. The more subtle dresses. It was difficult with the staff milling about. I had to put them amongst my own laundry just to get them out the door.

On the night of the ball Lilly will not be working so she will sneak out the servants door and wait by Anna's tomb. When the time is right I will feign with an illness which will send me back to the cottage. From there we will take the row boat I bought from Les to the city. We will spend the night at James Wilkes' before taking a coach to London then on toward Yorkshire and hopefully sanctuary of Charles' estate. I am hoping that Charles will be there waiting for us.

I have no fears of this plan not working. It will work. It has to work. Doesn't it?

I should leave with Lilly shouldn't I? It is the right thing to do. She should not stay here and can not travel alone. I should not stay here.

Still, what will become of my Duchess should I leave? She needs me.

Those words still ring in my mind from so long ago. *'**Their lives depend on me staying here with her'***

I don't know anymore.

It does not escape me how close to Halloween we sit with the ball this evening. Though it is still a fairly new concept in England to celebrate as wildly as our American cousins. They do appear to enjoy it. The day here is marked more by children than by adults. Perhaps all the ghouls and goblins will visit with us this evening. What a thought. If you had asked me a year ago if any supernatural being was real I would have laughed in your face. Not even my aunt's ramblings could have or ever did persuade me of this idea. It turns out I should have listened to her more closely.

As I sit here now with the fresh news of her death I can not help and wonder if I did her wrong. Maybe if I had not been so involved in my own life I would have taken the time to really listen to her stories. I was a child when my mother and sister died. We were told by the peelers, the local police force; that it was a break-in by a disgruntled ex-worker. My aunt never agreed. She was there that night, staying in our house. Father always insisted that break in was the cause of her brain breaking the way it did. The stories never made sense to me then, not that I have any more understanding now.
"Dark spirits" She would call them. "Red eyes, fingers like claws," Vague descriptions, "They took all the light from the room, blackened the globes and our minds. Voices echoing in our minds, still they echo to me. Tell me why I survived."

The words she spoke after this, it was the first time she made my father scared. A priest was called to our home. He was governed with expelling the demon my aunt believed had taken possession of her body. I was sent away, back to school before it began. Father told me only that he listened to her screams of agony, until she could scream no longer. The priest retired not long after and I knew nothing about him to ask his story.

One holiday from school I secretly went to her room, father had not touched it after she was taken away. It sat the way the priest had left it. An oppressive room to begin with stood then with every corner upturned. Only the bed remained in its proper place. The only clue I had to what happened was pure chaos. Heartbreaking to my immature mind.

I felt the same way as I stood outside Anna's bedroom. Cassandra wanted something from inside, though she did not feel strong enough to go alone. She held my hand while Mrs Lipton unlocked the door. A strange feeling came over me when it opened. I could not describe it at the time, fear, excitement, both? My heart beat sped up inside my chest. I had to clench my free hand into a fist to keep it from shaking. The ascent to the room was rickety, every step creaked without weight. I waited at the door while Cassandra shifted around the room. My eyes drifted to the yellow bed. My vision blurred with tears.

"I know it is still so terribly sad." The Duchess stood before me, squeezing my arm. "You made such an impression on our dear Anna. I think it was the first time she had smiled in years."

I blinked the tears away, only one fell, betraying me.

"Its, I don't, you say this and yet I barely remember our interactions. All of it is so fogged in my mind. In truth I don't think I could truly even describe her face and yet I feel as though I have lost a family member."

Her hold on my arm tightened.

"The past months have been tough on you. I am sorry your employment with us has been so strenuous." she reached her body up to kiss my cheek. I felt her body stiffen.

"Well, I have what I wanted, we should get back down stairs. I need to see the decorations are done correctly. Will you join me for a spot of tea in an hour?" she said.

I could not really refuse her. If my plan to leave was to succeed she must believe everything is normal. I left her and sneaked outside through the conservatory doors, making sure I was hidden by the plants inside. I sunk to the ground. I could see my cottage from where I sat, Marcoff was staring back at me from the bedroom window. I wondered if anyone else could see him there.

"This house, this Island is full of ghosts, is it not?" Mr Lipton towered over me.

"I um, I suppose all old houses do." I answered.

"Walk with me, sir." He turned before finishing his sentence. I pushed myself up and followed the Butler. He said nothing to start with, until we were a good way from the house.

"You understand duty well, Mr Whitman." He said.

"Yes I suppose I do."

"Your only duty in this house is the safety and ongoing management of the Duchess' finances. By now I would assume you are aware that Duchess Cassandra has this Island as her duty. Every person who lives here and the buildings are hers to care for. The house especially. This house is alive. Every wall can tell a story much older than you could imagine. The house is as much her duty as the Duchess is the house's duty. They are truly tied to each other and we are tied to them both."

I stopped us from walking.

"Does anybody here talk in anything other than riddles? No matter who I ask the answers are never the same and I-" The Butler's hand came up between us.

"Years of lying does that. You have found the journals, take heed of their words. It will help you."

I nodded, though I could not tell you the point of the conversation. It seemed like everyone wanted to warn me yet no one would tell me what against. He had given me no new information, none that I could decipher at that moment. We walked back to the house, him leaving me in the parlour. I looked around me at the room. Pink wallpaper had begun to peel between wooden panelling. A layer of dust had come to rest over most of the ornaments; far too much dust. I wondered who they would hire to clean once Lilly and I have gone. One person is not enough to clean the whole house, two maids at least would be needed, to even keep the main living areas tidy. An odd thought to have when I was hoping to never see the place again.

Cassandra came in whilst I was lost in my thoughts.

"Ahh Horatio you are here already." She was carrying a tray of tea. "I made it myself; with the cook watching me, of course." Cassandra bragged, placing the tray on the small table between us.

"The last month has been just awful for you, I know, still for me I have never had such a lovely time." She spoke as she poured out two cups of tea.

"It has been...Cassandra I want you to, to be happy, no matter what happens." She put the tea pot down forcibly. She passed a cup to me. "I may not always be around here, I mean my work may one day take me away from here."

Cassandra smiled.

"I don't think I will have to wait too long for your return. Please drink your tea."

I sipped the overly sweet drink. Perhaps she had forgotten that I didn't take sugar in mine. I did my best to not show any distaste.

"You did well, My Duchess." I said.

"Excellent! I shall tell the cook to leave immediately." She giggled behind her hand. I suppose the rest of our tea went well though I do not recall much of it, laughter is key in my mind. The jokes and anecdotes do escape my memory. I have returned to the cottage to get ready for the ball. It has been around three hours since our tea. I feel, I feel, well I feel happy. I cannot wait to get back up to the house. The ball will be such a lovely evening.

The Ball was wonderful.

I was introduced to several lovely people. Men who wore their hair down and long. An American called Lois told me how he had travelled across the ocean but saw the water only at night. All his stories were at night actually. I wondered if he was allergic to the sun. I have heard the affliction affects more people than we realise. Throughout our conversation I felt like his face was wrong in some way, like he had too many teeth for his mouth.

With him stood several men, all of them wore extremely nice suits, silk waistcoats and expensive watch chains; some of them had many medals on their chests. One wore a French medal from the war against Napoleon, the French medal of Honour. I was certain he could not have been alive to receive it, he would have to be over ninety years old; yet there he stood looking hardly over forty. The General dismissed me easily and without much thought. I suppose a lawyer is not worth the trouble. He was not alone, at the beginning of the night most of the guests treated me in a similar way. Of course to them I was no more than a lawyer, an employee of the Duchess. I know that would all change this evening.

The little lights were twinkling above us. I heard the awe of the guests, when they were turned on. All of us watched the ceiling for a few minutes until Mr Lipton banged a wooden mug against the staircase.

"Duchess Cassandra Whetton!" A door opened at the top of the stairs and the Duchess stepped out. She was wearing an elaborate black and blue dress that hugged her every curve precisely. Her hair had been curled and pinned and adorned with moments that sparkled in my eyes. I watched, open-mouthed as she smiled down at her guests. They all applauded her, Mr Lipton nudged me. I ran up the stairs, taking her arm in mine. We made a slow, deliberate descent down, moving purposefully to the middle of the dance floor. I bowed slightly as the orchestra began to play. I glanced at them, noticing how their skin appeared a pale shade of green in the darkened corner. We took hold of each other and began to dance.

The waltz was an intimate dance between two people. Our bodies close, touching yet still apart. After a few moments other couples joined us in the dance. Our eyes kept meeting until we could no longer pull them apart. As the dance came to an end, the guest applauded once more, this time to the orchestra. For the most part the ball was no different to any other I had been too. I danced with three other women throughout the evening. All of them danced as if their feet hardly touched the ground. For much of it I was caught up in the atmosphere of the night. Music playing, guests chatting around us. Any heavy thoughts I had previously worried about were gone. I was happy, happy to have Cassandra beside me.

I heard a bell ring, the chimes of the clock. I excused myself from the festivities, complaining of a headache and the need of air. Though concerned for me Cassandra had no qualms with my leaving and agreed that she should stay with her guests. I did as promised for the young maid. Not entirely as we had planned before. I met her at the tomb, walking with her to the boat. She would have to row it herself. I had known throughout the day that there would be no way for me to go with her now. I placed her suitcase into the boat along with a small locked chest. The keys I had sealed in an envelope and tucked into her hands.

"You must keep these safe. Take them, they will be of use when the time is right." The journals would be safe with her. "I am sorry Lilly, I would go with you to the end of the world if I was able, unfortunately I have made a promise that I must keep here. Marcoff will stay with you, he will protect you." The ghost burst once more into white flames beside the girl. She hardly flinched at all. Spirits were no new concept to the maid. No more words were spoken, she simply nodded. I wish I could have said the right word to her. I could have made her feel better about it all, perhaps. It was not something I could do. In fact my body had me already back in Cassandra's arms. I watched for a moment as she rowed away from the Island after I had pushed the boat away from the shore. With that girl all my hopes of a life off this Island were gone.

I ran back to the house, my chest tightening, still affected by the fire. As quietly as I could I snuck through the servants door. Mrs Lipton met me, her face was taught and her eyes scorned me.

"You have been gone too long?"

"It couldn't be helped. Do you have it?" I asked, still trying to regain my breath. Pressing her lips together, the housekeeper placed a small box in my hand. She took me by the shoulders, straightened me up, then nodded.

"Will she agree? It has been such a short time and her friends do not seem to like me much?"

With a raised eyebrow she laughed and walked away from me. I took in a long breath and returned to the ball. The room was jovial, all the guests drinking from the plentiful wine. I found Cassandra standing with the Transylvanian count and his four wives. Each of them were young and beautiful, their smiles wide as I approached. I am unaware of Transylvanian customs so I allowed their kisses and groping hands as they greeted me. The Count however, still showed his disdain for me. I ignored him, pulling the Duchess away, leading her to the staircase. I had her stand on the bottom step. The Butler gave the signal to the orchestra to silence. Cassandra looked around sheepishly to her guests.

"My Duchess, your Grace,"

"My Lawyer."

"Before my mother's death she made me promise her one thing, that one thing I have not been able to fulfil until this day. From the moment I arrived at this house I have felt the beauty of your soul in my heart. Your face is in my mind stopping me from thinking or working or being. I kneel here before you now, in front of all these people with this ring. A jewel passed to me through a blood line from the Royal family. With this ring and my whole body I ask you earnestly, Duchess Whetton, Cassandra, will you marry me?"

The murmur that went through the room at my blood link to the royals did not go unmissed by me. Cassandra looked away from me briefly, meeting Mrs Lipton's eyes as she stood by the doors. I saw her head bow. The Duchess turned back to me, a tear falling from her eyes. "Nothing would make me happier, Horatio." I slid the emerald onto her finger before kissing her hand. The guests behind me all burst into cheers and applauded once more. In that moment I had sealed my fate forever and I knew it.

I should be telling you why I did this, why I ignored everything I wanted yesterday and started this inevitable spiral to my death. For now though I will sleep and enjoy my last night as a man free from demons. Free in this cottage.

It has been long and I have been absent. The night after the ball was not as happy as I had originally thought. I have not survived it. Not in the way a man simply returns to the way he was before the event. This journal is almost filled, just as perhaps my life now comes to a close. I dictate these words to Mr Lipton as I am unable to use my own hands. He now will explain my plight.

It is with great sadness that I take over the words in this book. For too long have I watched the men of this house scribble their thoughts on the pages of journals that will not be understood. Too long have I stood by and let it happen before me, so many times. Always the same way. Not this one. This man has been different from the start. I wish I could have stopped it all but then I would have killed my wife in a way. These pages however are not for my pathetic laments.

On the night of the ball the guests were housed across the Island in cottages and rooms fit for each of them. We could have no idea when the lights were doused that one guest had an idea of their own. The lady was new to us, married into the Counts family amongst his other wives. Her lust for the life blood was still new and uncontrolled. The Count was too busy with his other mares to notice her disappearance.

None of us heard, could have thought a newly promised man would be in danger from another woman. Not even one that hides in the night. She broke into the cottage as easily as water seeps through cracks to come upon him. Her footsteps sounded like nothing more than wind drifting up the stairs. Her breath was silent as she reached across Horatio's sleeping body.

With gentle fingers she ran her hand down his nightshirt, the nail cleanly slicing through the thin cotton. The cold chill on his skin woke him. He had no chance to stop the first attack. Roxanna plunged her teeth into the skin below his right nipple. Haretio called out in pain. With a surge of strength a person only gets when they are in danger, he shoved the woman to the ground. He grabbed the gun he had left on his bedside.

Roxanna lunged for him, the first shot forced her back to the opposite wall. He wasted little time in running for the stairs, skipping several and hitting into the wall at the bottom. The book I had given him weeks ago had been fruitful. The knowledge in there had given him the knowledge to run from the woman. He knew he could not stop her. Simple bullets could not slow her down for long. The pale blue of her night dress appeared to glow in the night. The shot had reached me in the house. I was still clearing the ball room when it alerted me. There is no reason as to how I could have known where the shot came from but my heart sank when I heard it. I ran for the front door. The young lawyer was running as fast as he could along the path. Roxanna behind him. She moved swiftly across the grass though her feet barely moved. I ran back inside grabbing a wooden handled umbrella. By the time I returned to the doorway Roxanna had caught up with Horatio pinning him to the ground. I rushed out towards them, caring nothing for myself, breaking the umbrella to create a sharp point. Horatio was struggling against her, yet his strength was no match for her and once more she bit into his flesh.

I shouted, or rather screamed at her to release him. Her glowing eyes met mine, blood dripping from her mouth.
"He is mine!" Her voice echoed in my ears, holding and holding me in place. I could do nothing but watch as the woman lifted herself and Horatio into the air. No wings, no help from machines, only the power

of her cursed blood lifted her into the air. Too high for any of us to catch her.

As I stood rooted in place the other guests and household staff had drifted out onto the lawn.

"This is why the Count so rarely is invited to our gatherings." Louis said flatly. "He has never learnt to control his brood." shaking his head the pale man returned to his room in the house.

By now Horatio had stopped fighting back, his body limp in her hold. Roxanna never let up her feed.

"Lipton, Wilkes has been informed." Cassandra stood beside me, her face wet with tears, I couldn't read the emotion she displayed.

"Does she have the power to stop her?" I asked.

"It is what she was built for." she answered.

The dark figure that approached from the shore came as if Cassandra's words had timed it. Ramla Wilkes walked with a speed that humans do not possess. Her head tilted to one side, looking up at the couple in the air. Ramla crouched her body down before leaping into the air, landing on Roxanna's back, breaking her grasp on the lawyer. The two women began to fight in the air as Haretio plunged down to us. Cassandra dove forward, catching her new fiance in her arms. A show of physical strength she would normally hide. We took him inside quickly. I left them in the parlour with my wife and returned to the commotion. Ramla pulled a Khepesh from behind her, a sickle shaped sword, using the blade to slice through Roxanna's neck. The head hit the ground at my feet. Ramla walked up to me, throwing the rest of the body on the ground.

"Clear these grounds by morning or I will be back." Her words were simple, and full of every threat. I nodded. We went inside, leaving the body as it was.

Cassandra was frantic.

“He has lost too much blood.” she was gasping through her sobs.

“I sent Louis to find someone amongst the mortal staff who has the same blood type.” My wife said flatly.

“You must stop inviting these bloodsucking animals to our home! You silly child! This could jeopardise everything for you, for us. After everything that has happened here.” I scolded the Duchess.

“Coming from you. Do you think I am unaware of your antics? Ensuring he meets James and Ramla, giving him books and talking behind our backs. I see it all, *We* see it all!”

“Yet here he is, of his own free will, asking to be your husband, to keep you safe.” I raised my voice. Cassandra turned away holding her hand to her chest. I knew the look, “Cassandra what did you do?” I asked, looking between her and my wife.

“He was planning to leave with the maid, you know it as did we.” Mrs Lipton said, “We had to stop him for the sake of every soul in this house.”

“Would it really be so bad for us all to die at last?” I asked, defeated by it all. I slumped into a chair.

“When my father killed that queen they sealed our fate, then locked themselves in an iron tomb so they could be together and never have to face what we would become.. They left me here alone, a monster, to suffer their sins.” Cassandra sat down beside Horatio, fresh tears streaming down her face, “In two hundred years I have felt nothing but hunger, no love for any man until this one. How can it be that this world would happen to send me someone who could reach through the curse and touch my heart?” She said.

“Your heart hasn’t beat in two centuries, it feels nothing.” Ramla moved across the room, folding her arms over her body. She was dressed in the traditional clothing of her Egyptian people, more flesh showing than I had ever seen on a woman outside the bedroom. Cassandra shook her head.

"I was prepared to follow our usual plans, when he arrived his hand was hurt. I dressed the wound, his blood got onto my skin and it was warm. Then when we touched, it was as if water had been thrown over me. Slowly with each day, each time we saw each other, part of me came back to life." She spoke to the room, keeping her eyes on Horatio, stroking his hair.

"Do you think he could break the curse?" I asked, not wanting to hope.

"I do not know." She said.

"If he dies we will never know." Ramla said, "Give him to me, I will take him to James, we will do what we can for him." Something unsaid went between Ramla and Cassandra, their eyes locked onto each other.

"Will you return him to me?" The Duchess said quietly.

"I did not leave Egypt and dedicate my life to the protection of mortals for you to flaunt the expected rules. A choice must be made and it will not be yours. I will take him to my husband. We can fix this man's body then his mind must be his own." Ramla stood with her back straight.

Reluctantly we all agreed. Louis entered to tell us a young footman was waiting to help give blood to Haretio.

"He has given consent of his own free will?" Ramla asked. Louis nodded his head to her.

There was a wave of people rushing about as transport to the shore and across it was sorted and Ramla, Horatio and the footman were gone. When we were then alone, the room felt cold and empty. No music played in the house, the lights had been turned off or blown out. A void swept over us. The Count assured us that Roxanna's body had been encased in her coffin, chained with silver and dropped into the ocean with no chance of ever resurfacing.

For the next three days we tried to continue as normal. Our guests slowly drifted back to their own homes and away from the Island. The count was one of the last to leave. His luggage was taken aboard a large boat and taken away across the water.

Mrs Lipton gave Cassandra's hand and a small squeeze.

"You are beloved amongst the immortals, you Grace. The slight against you will not go unpunished. The Count comes from a bloodier time, but he will get his comeuppance." There was an attempt to comfort her though I could see it was not working.

The Duchess spent her days either sitting in her room or wandering about Horetio's cottage. We had all thought it right to pack up the place. Mr Whitman would be moving into the house when he regained his health or the worst would happen to him and us. Cassandra wanted so much to be in the presence of his things in hopes she could be close to him. She had taken to carrying his pocket watch inside her bodice.

"A boat is coming up from the mainland." My wife's words broke my thoughts and the Duchess'. I noticed the book she was holding.

"Why did you do it? Work so hard against me?" she asked.

"Two hundred years is a long time to be unhappy, I wanted only for this one to be fully informed. I thought, no I had hoped if he knew it all and still chose to stay this time would be different. I thought perhaps if you couldn't love you could at least find joy in him. I could never have dreamed that you and he both would develop true feelings for each other. Just as you could not anticipate this disaster of Anna getting to him." I felt my chest falter with emotion.

"Where is Charles?" she asked.

I let out a long breath, sadness had taken hold of this island, I wondered if we would ever get through it.

"He thought it best to make room for your husband. Charles had learned to truly love you in his own way. It hurt him to see this happen again. Do not forget he was here to watch Lord Gunther whittle away into an angry, bitter shell of the person he first met. He knew what jealousy would do to him. What you would do in front of him. How he would become what his predecessor had."

"Tell me where he is!" Cassandra demanded.

I hesitated for a moment, chewing my tongue."

"I do not know for sure, I was not privy to his full plans, but I would think has returned to the home of his family."

"Yorkshire?"

"Yorkshire." I agreed.

She stood from her chair moving across to the window.

"And his daughter? Lilly? Her absence has not been lost on me." Bitterness bit at every word.

"Gone to meet him I assume. As we should meet our guests."

Cassandra walked with me away from the cottage and back to the main house, where we were met by James and Ramla. They stood in the middle of the parlour with Horatio in a wheelchair. Cassandra ignored them and crouched before her fiance.

"How is he?" I asked.

"We have given him enough blood to restore an elephant. His mind is clear enough, in fact I have never seen a man with more conviction. Unfortunately the body is not as strong. He shows no signs of regaining physical health." James said.

Ramla stepped up to him, placing a hand on Horaio's shoulder. He looked up to her from Cassandra.

"Mr Whitman has to make a hard choice. We have given him all the advice we can. It is up to you now to inform him of your place and give him all the information of who you are and what will happen to him. Cassandra I need you to be strong at all times."

James pulled me aside.

"We have a way of healing him, the coven who cursed you all are still around. They have agreed to help you all. They cannot undo the magic but they can make him as the Duchess is." he whispered.

"Why would they agree to that?" I asked.

"Times have changed, they are not the same women who were hurt by Cassandra's parents. Also some may have a vested interest in the lads survival."

The pair gave us many more warnings about our choices of friends before leaving us. Mrs Lipton and I thought it pertinent to give the Duchess some time alone with Horatio. Still I chose to keep an eye on them. A vent in the wall made it easy for me to sit in the kitchen and listen to their words.

"I am so sorry, my love, for everything you have endured here." She took his hand in hers.

"Duchess, Cassandra please don't be like that, I could have left at any time. I stayed. For you I stayed." he said weakly.

"Why?" she asked.

"Cassandra I tried to not love you. I tried to turn my own head and find it in another person, but even when I was with her it was you. I thought about you all the time. It is as if our bodies have always known each other. How is it that we both are related to the royals? How could it be that we would find myself working at the firm that held your accounts? Why would they send me here? Our worlds have been spiralling to collide all this time. None of it could be a coincidence, surely?" His words came out breathy, as if his chest was straining to breath.

"You are a remarkable man, Mr Whitman. I will never understand how I deserve you."

"I am tired, my love. Perhaps you could read to me whilst I rest a little." he asked.

It was not until the next day that Cassandra chose to explain everything to Horetio. The three of us sat down together in the family room, with Horetio sitting across from us. I helped him out of the wheelchair and onto the couch. I looked at him, sitting there, pale; Mr Whitman had always been pale, a job that keeps you inside all the time will do that; yet now his skin seemed almost transparent. Every vein could be seen across his face and neck. Shame filled me, his vacant eyes looking at me without seeing me.

"Start at the beginning, tell me everything," he said.

"It started with a trip, a holiday for Cassandra's parents, at least that is what we thought. Their marriage was still new, their acquaintance had been short. None of us knew what he was truly part of. We were a new staff to the newlyweds. All we had been told was that the Duke was a war hero. The staff knew nothing of the organisation the Duke had been a part of. An organisation preparing for the trip for years. Not much is known of the details, they have been lost in time. You are aware of the village owned by the family in Egypt. That village is built above an underground system of tombs and halls. It was once lost to even the Egyptians themselves. Hidden by the priests of old that had worked so hard to keep the horrors away from mortal men. They believed the time of Gods and demons had run its course.

"The men involved with the organisation had gathered in the halls. In the darkness with only a few candles they prepared for a ritual. The ritual was as ancient as the halls they stood in. Alas the men had got the translations wrong. They thought they would be bringing forward a power of the Gods that would give them ultimate power over their futures. A power that would keep them all in wealth and nobility, here in England; perhaps the whole world.

"The ritual called for a young girl to be slaughtered, her blood spilled onto the sandstone. Unfortunately, the girl was the innocent woman they had hoped for and so the Gods they called to were left with a sour taste in their mouths, what they awakened with the girl's blood was horror. A Demon, for want of a better name, came amongst them, it ripped through the men of the order, tearing through their souls and replacing the good with, not bad, not evil, just something else. The Duke stood his ground, he took up the sword of the old priests and he took that demon into him. His body was wracked and it laid there for 3 days in a cave until he awoke once more. Around him his friends lie around him, like dogs waiting for their master." I took in a long breath and my wife took over.

"The woman they had taken and killed was the reason it went wrong, her name was Malinda Myers and she was of no simple virtue. The mistake was cutting the throat of a witch. Once back in England the men were beasts rampaging through the streets of london. Ramla calls them Jackals."

Horetio turned away from her, looking between us all again. "She said she is as old as the pyramids. How?" He asked.

"She is part of, well they clean up messes made by unnatural things." Cassandra said, "An order designed to lie in wait for the monsters of their religion to come alive. Ramla, she had awoken not long after the beast had. She followed my father here"

I twisted my pocket watch in my hands. "The Jackals were letting their inner natures control them, killing whomever they pleased, whenever they pleased. Unknowing of the Coven that tracked their movements, Ramla found them and they worked together. For twelve nights they hunted the Jackals and with their magic heightened with the Khepesh sword each night stunting the beasts inside until it was nothing more than a story in their blood. Ever since then they have kept the families under watch. For two hundred years they have kept watching."

"And the Duke?" Horetio asked.

"Nothing could be done to save him the way they saved the others. He was different from them. A choice had to be made by the Coven. A split in the power that had taken over him, so it could never be used again." Mrs Lipton explained before we all fell silent. His eyes swept the room again landing on the Duchess.

"So they, they moved it between your parents, you and the staff?" He eventually asked. Cassandra nodded ready to answer when the Lawyer coughed. The cough rattled his chest. I jumped forward holding onto his back and chest hoping it would help any pain he was feeling. A small line of blood left his mouth.

"This is too much for him!" I said.

"No, I'm fine, tell me." He waved me off, though I only sat beside him.

"Not just the people, the spell, something happened during the spell that changed it, the power seeped out into the house, the walls, the rooms, the Island. Nothing was spared." Tears fell from the Duchess' eyes.

"And now they are coming here again. Will they put it right?" He asked.

The air was heavy, as if smoke was filling the room. Horetio looked around him, I saw the realisation in his eyes.

"I have never seen this room before. Where are we?" He asked.

"It is the family room. A safe place. The rest of the house cannot reach this place." I said.

"It may not be as safe as we hoped." Cassandra had stood, her eyes looking up to the ceiling. Black smoke had begun to seep in through wooden beams. "We need to move now!"

I scooped Mr Whitman over my shoulder. Ignoring the painful groans he let out. My wife rushed with Cassandra to the back.of the room, they pushed against the wall until it moved back, a rush of cold air hit us all as we slid into the revealed passageway.

"What is happening?" Horetio asked over my shoulder.

"The damned, the spirits of people taken by the Jackals come back to this plane. They come to take the Jackals back to the land they come from. Returning them to the tomb in Egypt. They have never been able to take the Duchess, but you, you they may take." Mrs Lipton explained as we rushed through the narrow passage.

I could feel the darkness coming up behind me, filling all the space there. I felt it licking at my ankle like an excited dog. First my wife's footsteps went away, followed by Cassandra's and then, then there it was, black, dark, loud and everywhere.

◆·——·◆———·◆

Too much happened in such little time no one had a chance to breathe. I am different now, clearer, I can write.

I couldn't tell you where I went, only what I felt when I was there. All around me people jostled about, all fighting against each other. Everyone was fighting to reach a destination no one knew of. In the next moment I was laid on the ballroom floor. My body aching in every joint. From somewhere I found the strength to sit myself up. Mr Lipton was by the staircase, resting his back against it and rubbing his head with his hands.

"What happened? How did we get here?" I asked. Cassandra rushed over to me, her knees skidding across the floor.

"You're here! You're alive!" she cradled my face, looking into my eyes.

"He is off the bloodline, the blood may be stronger in him than we hoped." I knew the voice. I turned to see Mrs Hobbs standing before a crowd of women; the Cosell sisters directly behind her. My old landlady walked towards me. "We are his watchers, the Jackal is more apparent in his blood. We knew it after the attack on his family home. The Damned." She explained her eyes on me the whole time.

"This is the Coven." James, who had so far gone unnoticed, stepped forward to introduce the ladies.

Though my mind still held the fog of confusion I knew, I know, I know I am not the cause of my mother and sister's deaths, yet still I am. "They came for my father and I, didn't they? The damned? But then why did they kill them? My sister didn't have the same blood as me?"

"No dear boy, she was not your fathers. The man, the worker who was fired, was her father." Mrs Hobbs told me.

"I, I need some time." I said looking at my legs.

"Mr Whitman, there is not much time." James tried to plead with me. I looked up to Mrs Hobbs.

"Everyone leave, Now!" I had never heard her with so much authority in her voice. The ladies of the coven moved first, slipping out of the ballroom without a sound. The butler pulled Cassandra away from me, following the others out of the door. I silently thanked my old landlady like a child looking up to his mother. When only she and I were left, she knelt down beside me.

"Mrs Hobbs, how did all this happen? I just wanted a normal life. I was a lawyer, I did it all the right way."

She grabbed hold of me, my head resting on her shoulder. It had been too long since I had felt such a comforting hold.

"I am so sorry my dear. I wished so hard that you would be free of all of this. I tried to keep you safe. I failed you." tears welled in her eyes, they welled in mine also. The pain and aches of my months on the island were all weighing down on me at that moment. I let it all out. Sobs wracked my body as the woman who had been the strongest female influence in my world held me. I could not control it. All the pain, all the confusion, I still didn't understand my place in all of this. Why did fate bring me here?

"I wish I could take all of this away from you." she spoke softly as we sat there. I pulled back to look at her. I truly looked at her. The way I had once seen her, an old woman who fussed about me, it was wrong. I was wrong. She wasn't old at all, no that wasn't it. She is older but her face doesn't hold the lines I used to see. Her eyes are bright, dark, deep; just like Cassandra's they held the knowledge of many years, years beyond that of my comprehension.

"Why are you here? You said you were protecting me, yet I have been close to death too many times. Now you're here, why?" I felt anger bubbling in my gut.

"Horetio, I am part of a very old Coven. I am a witch. My powers can help you. Depending on your choice we can either ease your passing or make you more."

"More? Passing?" Panic took over the anger. "Ramla talked about something, the blood, when I was; when James was-"

"We should get off this cold floor, Horetio, we can discuss it further when we are comfortable. Can you stand?" She had distracted me, I knew it somewhere in the back of mind I was screaming at her, yet there I was anchoring my hands to the ground and pushing. My muscles shook under the strain. The stitches that held my skin together pulled apart. I am sure the one on my left arm had split completely as warm blood began to trickle down my arm. My breath stopped without permission. Mrs Hobbs held me under one arm trying to help me to my feet. Those feet slid out from under me and I fell back to the ground. The air rushed out of my lungs.

"I can't, I..." My eyes closed, rolled backwards and I couldn't control the coughing that once more took hold of me. I was trying to regain my strength though it did not feel like it would. Small hands reached down around me, lifting me. The scent of lavender filled my senses and I knew it was Cassandra who carried me. I kept my eyes closed. No, I had no control over them, over any part of my body. I knew what was happening. I had never been a man of God, in fact I had visited a church unless for a marriage or funeral in quite some time. Still here I was contemplating if I should make peace with the God I was told looks down at us from above. People talked all around me. Gently Cassandra placed me down, I finally opened my eyes. We were no longer in the house, a cold wind whipped round me as my wheelchair was pushed over the grass.

"Where are we going?"

"To the chapel. It is not connected to the house so we should have some protection there." Cassandra replied to me. I coughed once more, I reached a hand to my mouth as I coughed, feeling the wetness in my palm as I looked down. Red. Blood.

"Ramla?" Cassandra's voice was panicked. The Egyption warrior looked down at me.

"We are running out of time. The sun will be going down soon, we need to move fast if we want the magic to work." She called out to everyone.

I do not recall much of what happened after that, my mind was slipping in and out of focus. At some point I saw James and the Liptons leave the chapel , shutting the door behind them. Strong arms laid me on the altar, the Coven circled me, each one lighting a candle.

Ramla's face came close to mine. I forced myself to focus on her voice.

"Mr Whitman, you need to decide now. Your body is about to die. In a few hours you will no longer be what it was yesterday but will be reborn into what has killed you. The blood drinker, a night stalker. Vile European monsters, you will live only for blood. We will not let this happen to you. You must make a choice. The witches can and will ease your passing to the other side, or I can use their magic and the Jackal inside you to bring out what hides in your blood but you will not be an animal."

I was trying to follow her words but they were not coherent in my mind.

"I don't want to be anything but me." I said.

"Then you choose death?" Ramla stood straight.

"NO!" The Duchess flew up to my side.

"Cassandra."

"No, Horetio, please I love you, I can't let you do this" I took hold of her hand.

"My Duchess, if you love me let me go. I would have stayed with you forever but not this way. I don't want to be hurt any more."

She was crying, her tears hurt me. I knew then that I did love her beyond the spells, beyond the supernatural. It was simply a man who loved a woman. Was it the love of a husband? I didn't know, I couldn't know. She could see it in my eyes, I knew she did. She kissed me, a true earnest kiss.

Reluctantly she let go of my hand and moved away from me. The witches moved in closer, closing the circle around me and shutting the Duchess out. Ramla stood beside me, laying the Khepesh blade onto my chest. Chanting began around me, I fell into a peace I had never felt. Not one of the witches could have foreseen what was happening elsewhere.

Far across the planet as witches fought to carry my soul to peace a darkness was rising. The Jackals were not happy. The village owned by the Duchess had been quiet until that moment. People were running everywhere. Beneath their feet, bodies of men long chained to their tombs. Their bodies now twisting and reforming into the beasts, the dark wolves of Egypt. Each of them hungry for flesh.

They came crashing out of the sand and dirt ripping apart any human that they came across. Newly dead spirits twisting into the damned souls, shifting through the plains of existence and death until they landed at the Jackal's home. To the house on the Island.

Cassandra watched as the souls of the damned blackened by death twisted in the air above her home.
"No. Ramla, we have to stop this!" She called back into the chapel. Ramla looked out at the sky. With a final glance at the coven and me she grabbed the sword from my chest and rushed out.
"We will do what we can." Mr Hobbs reassured her.

Mr and Mrs Lipton smiled to each other; a smile that spoke of excitement. At the same time they began charging toward the house, their bodies twisting into a wolf-like creature. Their long snouts biting at the spirits, the black smoke breaking and screaming at their touch. A fight between monster and spirit raged whilst inside the chapel the ritual continued.

I had gone. My soul no longer in my body, no more pain, at last I was at peace, ready to go into the world beyond this one. Ready until a face appeared in front of me. First old, then slowly the wrinkles smoothed out until the young face of Anna faced me, smiling. She opened her mouth and that song I had felt in my muscles began to fill me. No, it was not just in my mind, she was there. Standing beside me, not standing. Anna was not in her human form, no her grey skin was almost as pallid as mine, her long tail wrapped around itself. Mrs Hobbs looked to the Cossel sisters who nodded to her. How had none of them heard the destruction of her tomb? It lay in ruins now, broken from the inside.

I had returned to my body, I knew it as every bite on my body was burning. The pain told me she was there, Roxanna. Her ocean soaked body limped forward, her mouth still stained with my blood. She approached me, silent yet screaming at me. Her cold, wet hands took hold of my feet, the burning pain disappearing in the same instance.

I heard Cassandra's footsteps at the door. Her red hair had turned black and her eyes were like fire. She moved swiftly to my side. Passing by the witches without touching any of them. A gust of sand blew about her feet. Where did the sand come from?

The three women stood now around me, like dark angels holding me to my body. A force, no one could see, pulled Mrs Hobbs closer to my head. Each of them held on to my body and I began to shake.

"Close in sisters!" Mr Hobbs called to the Coven. Each of the witches stepped forward at the same time. Their bodies now touching shoulder to shoulder, the latin chants echoing around the chapel. I do not know how it looked to them, but for me, I felt a beam of white light leave the chest of the four women, pouring into me.

In the darkness of the void of death I felt my wounds heal to scars. The strength of my muscles returned. The siren's song worked its way into my voice box, settling there its new home. Above us all the moon shone down full and bright, it warmed my skin as if I stood below the midday sun. I no longer felt weak, no longer was my mind confused. I was strong and fixed and glorious.

Time went by without my knowledge, when I finally opened my eyes I was alone. I pulled the white cotton sheet, covering my face, away and slid off the altar. They thought I was dead. Of course they did, I had no heartbeat to speak of, no warmth to my skin. I looked around myself. The little chapel existed only as a dream in my new vision. It shifted in and out of view. My feet stepped but felt no weight on the ground. I know I pushed the door open but I could not feel it. The sun above me, burnt my eyes at first, sending a golden glow around everything I glanced at. Around me I could hear the trees swaying in the gentle breeze, my tongue could taste the spices in the air, coming from the mainland. My senses were working on overdrive and it felt...it felt wonderful. Fresh and ancient all at once.

I looked up at the house seeing how the spirits of the damned wrapped themselves in a black smoke around the roofs and spires. Mr and Mrs Lipton sat defeated on the grass, the husband holding his wife. Their eyes grew wide when they saw me. Instinct had them following me.

"Mr Whitman you're alive?" The Butler called out to me.

"You could say that, I may be more alive now than I ever was or I could be more dead." I continued to walk as I talked. A tinge of another voice layered over my own.

The door to the manor house opened before I reached it. A ruin standing with no glory of its former self.

"Horatio?" The voice was like a song to my ears.

"Cassandra."

The Duchess was standing at the top of the stairs; her dress torn and dirty. My legs moved me to her side in a second. I took hold of her hands in mine.

"How?" She whispered the question.

"Too much magic from too many Gods. This is what happens." Ramla stepped out from a room downstairs, holding her husband, James, up. "The ancient Gods of Egypt, the old pagan Gods of England housed together in that Christian hovel. It was a conduit." She explained. I smiled down at the Duchess.

"They are inside me, Roxanna and Anna, their powers are here. Yours and Mrs Hobbs I feel you all, hear the words of magic dancing inside me. Mrs Hobbs? Where is she?" panic hit me.

"It's okay, she is safe." Cassandra's hand on my chest calmed me. Those words were all I needed, at that moment. Neither of us noticed as the Wilkes made their leave. I saw the sadness in her eyes and nothing else. My heart knew how to make her happy.

"Come my love, let us rest now, just for a little while and when we wake, our home will be as beautiful as you."

She followed my lead to her bedroom, all the while the house breathed a sigh of relief as new life sprang into the bricks. Before closing the door I glanced upward, seeing the spirits through the broken roof and I spoke, "Incipiunt quieti" silver orbs of light engulfed the blackened spirits until the sky was clear above us.

It has been almost two years since I looked at this journal. So much has changed. The ghosts of the past still linger amongst us. Cassandra's first three husbands still wander the grounds, their spirits tied to the magic that captured them. Still now they smile, no longer saddened by their plight.

Anna's tomb has been rebuilt though only a stone siren resides inside. With her power transferred to me her body broke and became a statue. I have learnt to use her voice in a new way. I do not sing, but no one can resist my commands.

The Butler and Housekeeper have been relieved of their duties and we have started building them a home on the far side of the Island. They can live out their lives as a free married couple.

As for the mainland and the people of England, they have forgotten us. My dear Mrs Hobbs helped to hide the Island from discovery and memory. Only those who know of the island can find it.

We are, it seems, at peace at last.

Word was sent to us from the Whetton Estate in Yorkshire, Mr Whetton had died. It appeared that being so far away from the Duchess had broken her hold on him and so his body aged rapidly. A peaceful death we are told, in his sleep with his daughter beside him. I have decided that I will go to his funeral. I will take this book with me. I would enjoy a moment with Lilly once more. She has the other journals so it is only right that she has this one as well.

Perhaps our stories will save someone in the future, or give them a wonderful idea for a book. For the last time I write my last words here. Goodbye until you, my reader, find me once more.

Duke Horatio Whitman.

EPILOGUE

"Hey Michael, what was Lilly's job before her father died?" The girl asked her brother,

"Umm, a maid, I think before she was married. I suppose he wanted her to get all of his money so had her marry a cousin." Michael replied.

Catrina closed the diary she had found in the attic, dropping it into the suitcase with several others. She took a long, deep breath.

"I'm going home, you'll be okay here?" she asked.

"It is my home now so I suppose I'll have to be. Give me a call when you get there." He kissed his sister's forehead before she left him in the attic.

Catrina skipped down the stairs, she stopped suddenly at the table in the entrance hall. A notebook sat there. She did not fully know why but something told her to take the book and the pens beside it. Her blue car was small and old but good enough for her. She threw the suitcase on the back seat and slid behind the steering wheel. Before driving away she wrote on the first page.

'My name is Catrina Harman. Today I read a diary. Today I discovered a truth. The old words of a Duke. A lawyer. A man. A monster?'

"Greater love has no one than this: to lay down one's life for one's friends" John 15:13

"Perhaps it is our imperfections that make us perfect for one another." Jane Austen.